SILENT PASSING

By Sid Perkes

PublishAmerica
Baltimore

First printing

This is a work of fiction. Names, characters, places, and incidents either are the product of the author's imagination or are used fictitiously. Any resemblance to actual persons, living or dead, events, or locales is entirely coincidental.

PublishAmerica has allowed this work to remain exactly as the author intended, verbatim, without editorial input.

ISBN: 1-60836-545-X
PUBLISHED BY PUBLISHAMERICA, LLLP
www.publishamerica.com
Baltimore

Printed in the United States of America

ACKNOWLEDGMENTS

Thanks and appreciation to my friends for their support and encouragement in the long writing and publishing process, especially to Marilynne Glatfelter and JoAnn Perkes.

I

The metal roller skate wheels clattered as they skimmed over the cracks in the sidewalk. The sound filled the early summer afternoon air. Andy rounded the corner, made a half turn and skated onto the grass. He adjusted his cap and fished in his pocket for the skate key as he made his way across the ribbon of lawn to the concrete milk can stand and sat down. It was no use trying to roller skate on this street. The damn poplar trees made it impossible.

The poplars that lined both sides of the street were past their prime. The gray gnarled trunks, now rotting and often hollow, held vertical a cluster of shafts with silver-green leaves that fluttered like sequins in the warm afternoon breeze. The trees that had not lost the constant struggle with spring winds rose to over fifty feet in height. Andy hated them. As the trees grew, their roots crept under and gradually buckled the sidewalks that lay between the rows of trees and neat picket fences protecting well-kept lawns from stray cattle. There were a number of stretches in town where the sidewalks were so buckled that nobody could skate on them or ride a bicycle, and people had a difficult time walking without stumbling.

Andy undid the clamp on his left skate, pocketed the key and removed the rubber canning jar ring that held the other skate securely to the sole of his shoe. The clamp on his right skate had been broken for two years, and the only way to hold the skate to the shoe was with a bottle ring. He buckled the ankle straps together, threw the skates over his shoulder and started down the street toward home.

As usual he and Ray had played too long out by the old canal, and he was late for chores. Catching hell for being late was a common occurrence. Things were different now that his brother Ned was off in the South Pacific fighting the Japanese because Dad depended on Andy's help with the chores more than ever.

The afternoon shadows cast by the poplars cut diagonal stripes across the sidewalk and lawns. Andy thought how nice it would be when the poplars were gone.

Many of the trees were uprooted or ripped apart by the winds this past spring, and there was talk that the town fathers would be cutting down and replacing all of them.

The town was filled with poplars. Dad said sometime back in the 1880s when the settlers knew the town was firmly established they decided it was time to beautify the streets. He didn't remember why the town fathers decided to plant poplar trees instead of oak, elm or even box elder trees; but they planted poplars on every east-west street of the town.

By the time Andy was born the trees were old. He didn't think they were of much use. They were no fun to climb because the branches were too brittle to support much weight, and there were no horizontal ones that he could make a swing on. They were pretty, sometimes. Riding toward town on the streetcar from the city, it looked more like a forest than it did a town. The houses, barns and even the silos were hidden by the rows of tall poplars. The town looked inviting, secluded and safe.

A bird about the size of a sparrow had built a nest in the hollow of one of the trees, and Andy was startled when she flew at him to warn him he was too close to her nestlings. He laughed as the small bird flitted and darted around his head chirping frantically. Two sure signs of summer were when the bird's broods hatched and when all the kids got out their roller skates. Only yesterday Andy retrieved his skates from a box in the basement and oiled them, and now the mother bird determined to protect her young. Summer was definitely here.

It was time to find some jobs to earn money during summer vacation, but with the extra responsibilities on the farm Andy supposed all he would have time to do would be a job driving cows. The grass was mature and by next week farmers should start taking the cows to pasture every day.

The grassland was mostly west of town on the lowland in the center of the valley. Dad said the lowland area had poor drainage and the ground was boggy and not fertile enough to raise corn or grain, but it was good pastureland.

Almost all of the farmers had a pasture west of town, and each farmer's herd of cows was driven to pasture each morning and brought back every evening from early summer until after the fall harvest. After the autumn freeze when the grass stopped growing the cows were wintered in the corrals and barns. A lot of the kids made their summer spending money by driving cows for the farmers who had no young boys of their own, and who were willing to pay the three to five dollars a month. The amount paid depended on the size of the herd and the distance the cows had to be driven each day.

Dad told Andy why the farmers hired kids to drive the herds. By paying kids to do the job, the farmers could stay in the fields for an extra hour or two before milking time and during summer they needed all the time in the fields they could get.

Depending on the location of the pastures, some kids were lucky enough to be able to drive two herds. The summer before last one kid found a way to drive three herds.

Last summer Andy's brother Ned took responsibility for driving Dad's herd so Andy could drive his Uncle Jed's cows and earn some money.

Ned left for the army last July and Dad took over the job. With Ned still away Andy would have to drive Dad's herd this summer, but he couldn't drive his Uncle Jed's herd too. The herds went to pastures that were down different roads. But he needed money, so if Dad would let him he would try to find a second herd that was pastured down by Dad's pasture.

He could make a lot more money by getting a job hoeing sugar beets or corn, but he couldn't hire out because he had to help with hoeing Dad's fields, as well as do all of his milking chores and haul hay.

He sure hoped Dad would pay him. Last year for his work on the farm Dad didn't pay him on a regular basis like he received from driving cows, but he did give Andy money last fall to buy some new clothes for school.

Andy took off his cap and brushed the blonde hair from his forehead. He adjusted the skates so the straps didn't dig into his sun-reddened and tender shoulder. He got the sunburn yesterday mowing the lawn, and his back was sore under his blue and white cotton pullover shirt. He replaced the cap on his head, stuffed his hands into his pockets and continued his trek home.

Andrew Parker was small for age eleven. Most would think him no more than eight or nine. His straight blonde hair, which was already beginning to sun-bleach even lighter as it did every summer, fell casually framing the thin regular features of his face. His eyes, which drooped slightly at the temples, gave him a fragile somewhat sad appearance; but they also held a twinkle and a mischievous look. His almost totally English ancestry was reflected in Andy's features and his skin, but unlike his sister Donna's, his skin tanned rather than freckled with exposure to the sun.

Andy had friends but spent most of his time playing by himself or with Ray. His mother was always trying to get him to spend more time with friends, but much of the time Andy preferred being by himself. That was one reason why he liked driving cows as a summer job; it was something he could do alone.

Last summer, he only made three dollars and fifty cents a month working for Uncle Jed because his uncle only had eight cows and his pasture was just a mile and a half away. Andy needed to find another herd. He didn't want to upset his uncle but Andy had to find a herd that took the same route as Dad's herd.

Dad's pasture was down the main road into town. It was west beyond the highway down the airport road just across the railroad tracks. That was on the other side of town from his uncle's pasture. If Andy were to drive a second herd it would have to be one that was pastured down the airport road. That way he could bring both herds home at the same time. Uncle Jed would have to understand things had to change because Ned was away.

Another reason to find another herd was because Uncle Jed's back barnyard fence separated his corral from the old man's corral, and Andy was afraid of him. The old man was really strange. His features were large and fleshy. His face sagged with age, and his nose and lips were overly large as were his jowls. The eyes were small and sunk deep under the heavy bushy gray eyebrows. He never smiled, and the expression on his face never changed.

Andy saw the old man sometimes when he was locking the gate of Uncle Jed's corral after bringing the cows home in the evening. He would be looking at Andy from his barn window. He just stared through the dirty pane with his old felt hat pulled low on his brow. The crown and hatband were stained where perspiration had soaked through. His large hands clutched the straps of his faded bib overalls. It made a shiver run up Andy's spine, and he would quickly jump on his bicycle and pedal down the lane as fast as he could. Andy felt as if he were being chased and could only breathe easy when he turned the corner toward his house.

The old man's name was Charlie and he lived just up and across the street from Andy's house. He was not afraid when he saw the old man working in his front yard, but there was something about being alone around him that scared Andy. Lots of stories circulated among the boys. Most said he was crazy, that he had never gotten over the shock of his wife's death some six or seven years ago. The adults never said much about him one way or the other, but he was someone the boys were very wary of. The older boys gathered in the evening after chores were finished and supper was over to play games, chase girls or tease some of the older townspeople who responded to the pestering; but they never teased the old man. If they left him alone it was for good reason.

When Andy was well past the tree, the bird made one last dive at him and flew back to her nest. Andy, conscious that he was daydreaming again, turned to see if anyone was watching him and to see where the bird had gone. His foot caught the edge of a buckled section of the sidewalk and he felt himself falling. Andy struggled to pull his hands from his pockets. He freed one but the other caught. In reaching with his free hand to break his fall, he let the skates slip from his shoulder and the jolt of their weight hitting his forearm forced it to his side. Things happened so fast. He heard a thump that seemed to come from inside his head. Everything went white and then all went black.

II

Charlie placed the end of the long-handled hoe under his arm, removed his sweat-stained felt hat and with a handkerchief from his back pocket he mopped the perspiration from his brow. The afternoon shadows cast by the house and trees crept steadily across the vegetable garden. Soon he would be in the shade, and with the breeze that came up every day in the late afternoon, it would be cooler and his task would seem easier.

For the past few years Charlie dreaded the coming of summer. He didn't know how long he could continue to farm. It was harder each year. Taking care of his farm and cows was hard during the winter, but with summer came the work in the fields and taking his cows to pasture, and in the fall the harvest. All of the tasks were made more difficult because of how the farms in the area were laid out.

When Charlie was a young man he learned the reason why the pioneers built the settlement the way they did. The plan for the town was not uncommon in the west before the Indian wars. It involved extra work but it functioned as they planned. The founding families were the first white people in a valley that was home or hunting grounds for several Indian tribes. Because of the threat of Indian attack it was necessary to have all the settlers' homes and barnyards clustered in a town instead of each family homesteading separate sections of land scattered around the valley.

The town, located in a mountain valley on the western slope of the Rocky Mountains, was nestled at the base of foothills on the east side of the valley. It was near the mouth of one of the many canyons that were

11

carved into the jagged mountain range by runoff from melting snow over countless winters.

Charlie heard the stories about the valley once being part of a great prehistoric lake that covered not only his valley but a good portion of the state. When the lake drained from the Great Basin into the ocean, Charlie's valley remained underwater until a breach in the mountains on the west side of the valley allowed the lake to drain into the great western desert.

The deltas formed by the streams emptying into that ancient lake were now the bench land at the base of the mountains, and the lake's shoreline was apparent on the lower face of all the mountains surrounding the valley.

A dozen small communities dotted the valley floor, each located near a large spring or the mouth of one of the canyons with a stream flowing from it. The streams provided the water necessary to sustain the people and irrigate the farms.

The city five miles south of Charlie's town was built at the mouth of the major canyon from which flowed the largest of the streams emptying into the valley.

Besides protection from the threat of Indian attack, there was a second reason for settling the town the way the pioneers did. The quality of the land on each side of town differed greatly. Homesteading a section west of town on the grassland would certainly have failed. The cattle would have good pasture in summer, but the land was so poor it could not produce enough hay and grain to feed the cattle through the winter; and the land was not fertile enough to grow corn or peas to provide the homesteader a cash crop. There was no way a farm west of town could succeed.

Homesteading a section of land east of town would also be doomed because of a lack of irrigation water. Even after the canal system was built much of the land east of town remained dry farm. It was only fit for growing hay and grain, and there was often only one crop of hay a summer. The orchards planted below the upper canal provided cash crops today but that was not the case when the town was settled.

Only the land north and south of town was capable of providing all the crops needed for a successful farm. The settlers decided the best course of action was to build a town and allot a parcel of land on each side of town to all the families.

Very little of the grassland west of town was used by the first settlers for several reasons. First, with so few people, there was plenty of land close to town to both farm and pasture the animals. Second, pasturing cattle and horses on the grassland so far away from town would make it easy for the Indians to steal them. And third, the settlers were so busy turning the fertile land into fields for crops that there was no time to build fences. By the time enough people had moved into town all the good land was needed for crops, the Indian wars were over, and it was safe to pasture animals on the grassland.

The town was laid out in square ten-acre blocks with eight building lots to each block. The one and a quarter acres provided ample room for a house with a garden behind it, a calf pasture, a corral, a barn and all the out buildings needed to support a family farm. A lane through the center of each block provided access to the street for all the barnyards. Because houses faced each other across the streets each family had a pleasant view of their neighbors' front yards from their living room windows. The barnyards were mostly hidden by fruit trees planted in the calf pastures and around the garden plots so they were usually not a part of anyone's view.

Later some houses were built on the north-south streets. They didn't have the best view. Often their living room windows overlooked someone's corral or barnyard. The later houses interfered with some of the lanes through the center of the blocks. Some were cut off halfway through and restricted access to the barnyards. That's what happened to Charlie's lane and was the reason he had to take his milk cans each morning to the milk can stand next to the street in front of his house.

The canyon streams emptied into the river that meandered through the low flatlands in the center of the valley. The Bear River flowed into the valley from the north and slowed to a deep, murky, creeping giant by the time it reached the flats, and spread across them as it took in the water from the mountain streams. Finally it made its way through the same breach in the western mountains that drained the prehistoric lake.

When he began farming, Charlie found the system easy and workable, but now he was old and the layout of the farm was a big problem for him. He struggled every day to find the strength and energy to complete his work in the fields and then walk the mile and a half to bring the cows home from pasture during summer. By the time he finished the morning milking and drove the cows to pasture, he was late getting to the field; and by the time he was finished in the field, drove the cows home, milked them and did his other chores it was almost dark, even on the long days of summer. It was exhausting. Life would be so much easier if he lived on a regular farm where the pasture was close to the fields and the fields were close to the barnyard, but he doesn't.

Charlie knows how much he needed help. He has to find someone to drive his cows to pasture. He knows he's too old to do everything by himself, but he doesn't know who to approach. To make matters worse he has no savings and no close family so if he stops farming he'll have to go to the poorhouse or starve.

From somewhere up the street he heard a bird frantically chirping. Someone was too close to her nest. He leaned against the hoe handle and watched for a moment the poplar leaves flutter silver and green against the clear afternoon sky. The mountains to the east were green and lush with an abundance of plant life that flourished each spring until the summer sun sucked out the moisture and life from the hillsides and turned them into a sea of yellow-gray grass and sagebrush. Only the pine and cedar trees on the south faces of the canyons and along the crest of the mountains remained green throughout the hot summer.

It was time to do the evening chores. He would finish hoeing after supper when the garden was completely shaded. He stuffed the handkerchief back into his pocket and walked to the milk can cart he parked each morning by the shed behind the house. Slowly he made his way toward the street to where his milk cans sat on the concrete stand next to the street outside his front gate.

He opened the gate and turned to pull the cart through when he saw the boy lying on the sidewalk a hundred yards up the street. Charlie went to his side as quickly as he could. At first he thought the boy was dead. Blood covered his face from a gash in his forehead, but he had a pulse. He gently lifted the boy who groaned and stirred as Charlie carried him to the daybed in his living room.

He knew the lad was the young Parker boy from across the street. There was something about the face of the unconscious boy that stirred memories in the back of Charlie's mind.

He placed the boy on a towel on the sofa and with a piece torn from a clean white dishtowel he wrapped the boy's wound to stop the bleeding. Through the lace curtains he saw the boy's sister coming down the street, and he hurried to the front yard, waved her to him and told her to bring her mother to his house.

Returning to the kitchen he drew a basin of cool water, threw the remaining piece of dishtowel over his arm and went in to wash the blood from the boy's face.

* * * *

Soap. Andy could smell soap. It wasn't on him; it was in the air. His aunt's house smelled of soap. He must be at her place. Her soap didn't have a clean smell; it had a strong one that seemed to be covering up some strange odor. Andy didn't like to eat at his aunt's house because everything tasted like the smell of that soap.

He slowly became aware that he was awake and not at his aunt's. The smell was different from any he knew. He struggled to sit up but became dizzy, and pain shot through his head. He laid back and blinked to clear his vision. Slowly the strange room came into focus. It was as if someone were adjusting the lens on a slide projector like the one they had at home.

Despite his aching head, Andy was fascinated by what he saw; the room was from the past. Across from the leather daybed on which he was lying was a huge sideboard, its top cluttered with small gold frames containing old photographs. He had never seen the people in them before. The photos had a brownish tone. They were tintypes like the ones of his grandparents and great grandparents on the low chest in his mother's bedroom. The people were posed in the same stuffy manner. Behind the photographs the wallpaper was a musty green with darker green designs; large floral patterns which were highlighted with antique gold.

Andy surveyed the rest of the room. There were two large armchairs with lace doilies pinned to the headrests and on the arms. The chairs were covered with a striped cut-velvet of the same musty green color as the wallpaper. He was lying on a leather daybed that seemed to be the same style as the armchairs.

The tables and the legs of the other furniture in the room were dark wood and heavily carved. The table legs had feet carved like animal claws which rested on the ornate carpet. The blinds behind the heavy lace curtains on the three windows above him were olive green and the light through them gave the room an eerie stifling feeling. The blinds were partially drawn and slivers of light darted across the room and cast an amber glow interwoven with busy shadows of lace curtains on the wall across the room. The room had a weird feeling about it.

Was it evening? Andy remembered that he fell, but he didn't know where he was or how he got here.

Across the room, a door with a tasseled portiere opened and Andy quickly closed his eyes. There was a quiet rustling noise and slowly Andy opened his eyes, peeking through his eyelashes to see who had entered the room. A person, with his back to Andy, wrung out a cloth in a basin of water. The water splashed back into the container. As if in a dream, the figure turned and slowly shuffled toward him. Andy's heart leapt into his throat. It was the old man and he had a strange smile on his heavy-lipped mouth. Andy tried to run as the old man reached the sofa. He was dizzy, his head shot with pain, his heart pounded, he tried to scream, the old man stopped smiling, his head spun, he heard pounding and everything went black.

* * * *

Charlie placed the unconscious boy back on the daybed and went to see who was knocking on his front door. The boy's mother and sister had knocked on the door just as the boy began his short, delirious outburst. The boy's mother kept apologizing for the incident as she carried him from the house and thanked Charlie repeatedly between apologies. He had seen the terror in the boy's eyes. He knew how afraid the boy was of him, and he knew the boy's mother was aware of that too.

Evening chores seemed to take longer than usual. The sun was setting when he returned to the house. Shafts of rose-colored light struck the tops of the poplars, cast long shadows up the street and turned the mountains east of town bright pink. There wasn't a storm approaching from the west so tomorrow would be another clear warm day.

He went to the front yard to find where the paperboy had thrown his evening paper this time, and the boy's mother met him at the gate with a fresh loaf of homemade bread. She had been watching for him. She thanked him and apologized again. The bread was a welcome addition to his meal.

The evening was cool and only a few slashes of red caught the edges of the wispy clouds hovering above the western mountains. He pulled the hoe through the loose soil cutting the rapidly growing milkweeds from between the still tender stalks of corn. The image of the boy's face filled his mind and again memories stirred in him. He had seen that bloodied little face before. Sometime. Somewhere.

III

Andy heard the doctor talking to his mother. The doctor said Andy had a mild concussion and had to stay in bed for two or three days at the least. They would see how things went. She was not to worry about the cut. It would heal fine. The stitches could come out in ten days. Andy touched the gauze bandage on his forehead. Under it he could feel a lump and made out five stitches.

The front door slammed and his mother came into the room. Emma Parker was a small woman. Her hair was pinned in a bun at the nape of her neck and it was prematurely gray. A few strands had pulled free from the bun and hung limply over her ears. Her clean print housedress and dress-up shoes told Andy she was expecting company long before she announced the doctor would be calling in the afternoon to check on his condition.

Yesterday, when Andy fell, Dad was working in the south field, but his mother didn't know how to drive the family car so she called the doctor and he drove to town from Lewisburg to tend to Andy's head. She had been frantic and had not cared about her appearance. Her dress had been soiled from the day's work and her apron pocket torn. It was only after the doctor left that she became embarrassed about how shabbily she was dressed, and Andy's mother was very concerned about appearances. She seldom went visiting, so having company was a special occasion, even if it was just a house call by the doctor.

Andy had noticed that when there was an event for his mother to attend she would be dressed and pacing hours before it was time to leave, and he thought his mother was different in another way too. Even though his dad and his sister were constantly around, Andy felt there were times when his mother was off in her own world. During those times it was as if Andy was not there. To him she often seemed to be lonely and searching for something.

He knew his mother's life had been one of hard work and total dedication to her husband and children. Andy had heard the stories. She was the oldest of a large family, and when she was fourteen her mother died and she was forced to quit school to care for the younger children.

Andy's mother and father grew up in the same neighborhood. Dad courted her for four years before they married when she was twenty. His mother said their courtship consisted primarily of sitting on the back porch swing after she put her siblings to bed. Because her father was sickly she had to always be around to care for her brothers and sisters. Andy knew that his mom and dad had occasionally gone to town dances, but she said the one or two dances a year were the only social events of their courtship.

Her father was unable to care for the two youngest children so when Emma married, her two brothers came to live with her.

Donna was born fifteen months after the wedding and Ned followed eighteen months later.

The years passed and the brothers married and moved away, and Dad spent longer hours in the fields as he acquired more land and with it more work.

Andy was a surprise. Everybody said so. He was born when his brother and sister were old enough to take care of themselves, and sometimes Andy thought his mother really didn't want to raise him. She never had time to have hobbies or develop a close circle of female friends. Her closest friends were the members of her bridge club, but they were really more acquaintances than friends. Outside the bridge club meetings she seldom socialized with the women. Since she was never very active in the community she didn't have much in common with the townswomen. Andy thought maybe that was why she seemed lonely and in her own world.

Emma Parker gathered pieces of gauze and tape from the night table and asked Andy how he felt.

"Okay I guess," Andy said, "but my head hurts sometimes."

"You'll have to stay down for a few days. Did you hear what the doctor said?"

"Uh huh."

"Do you want anything?"

Andy glanced at the table next to the bed. There were pills, orange juice, water and comic books, although he wasn't supposed to read for very long.

"Can I have some ice cream?" He asked, "It's hot in here."

"We don't have any and I don't have time to go to the grocery store right now. Maybe your father will get you some if he finishes his chores before the service station closes."

She put the back of her hand to Andy's forehead and, satisfied he had no fever, she left the room.

There was no use asking again because his mother was about to put the bread dough in the tins to rise before baking. It was two-thirty and the bread went into the oven at four o'clock every day. Andy loved the smell of bread baking, but he loved the first slice of hot bread more. He couldn't have that first slice until Donna got home.

Donna worked as a maid in the city. During her high school years she took the streetcar to the city each day after school, worked until 6:00 pm and came home on the 6:20 train.

Before Andy was old enough to go to school, he would stand on the sofa so he could see out the window and wait for the streetcar. When the 6:20 stopped at the corner up the street and he saw Donna coming down the street, he would be in the kitchen pestering his mother to cut the bread. His favorite was the crusty end of the loaf with lots of butter and jam.

Andy read that streetcars were the best way to travel in big cities, and he thought it was strange that his small town had one. Andy loved trains so he asked his teacher about the streetcar. She said it was really an electric train system, but that most people in the valley called it a streetcar. It had been around for a long time. When the system was built, there weren't a lot of cars in the valley, and the road through the canyon out of the valley was terrible. The train was a great way to travel and lots of people used it.

His teacher told him about the other train line that ran through the valley, the one that used steam engines and pulled a lot of railroad cars. The tracks came into the valley through a breach in the mountains on the west side of the valley-the same gorge that allowed the prehistoric lake to drain into the desert. There were two parallel sets of rails through it, one set for the train and the other for the electric streetcar. The Bear River also flowed out of the valley through the gorge, and the tracks were laid along the riverbank. The steam train only made stops in the city and the big town to the north. It took passengers all across the county.

The streetcar line went through most of the towns in the valley. It went from a big town in the north end of the valley, which was in another state, all the way to the state capital; which was about a hundred miles to the south. His teacher said the train system was actually two lines joined together. Some people down state in the capital city built a line north to the state's second largest city, and a man who lived in the city in Andy's valley built the line from the second largest city to the big town in the north end of the valley.

Andy had ridden on it to the city many times, but he had never been out of the valley on the train. He loved watching the trains. Someday he wanted to ride the streetcar all the way to the state capital, and when he grew up he wanted to travel all around the country.

Since she graduated from high school Donna worked full-time during the day and arrived home on the 5:20 streetcar. She was engaged to be married in August when her fiancé Mike came home on leave from the army.

Andy thought Mike was nice. He was tall, had a strong jaw, an olive complexion and black hair. Everyone said he was extremely handsome, but Andy thought Ned was the better looking of the two. Mike was three years older than Donna and was from a town on the west side of the valley. His father owned a general store where they sold groceries, dry goods and even toys. Mike often brought Andy a gift when he came to see Donna so Andy liked to see him come visiting. Mike was drafted about the same time as Ned, but he was stationed somewhere in the south and had not seen overseas combat.

Donna and Mom spent most evenings sitting on the porch swing crocheting edges on pillowcases and sewing things for Donna's hope chest.

Andy remembered the stories he heard about Donna when she was a kid, and it was hard for him to believe she had really been a tomboy. Donna was gangly when she was young, at least that's what Andy heard from the stories told by his parents; but he only remembered her after she reached her teens. His mother said Donna was a handsome girl who would blossom into a beauty as she grew older, and his father said her body had finally caught up with her feet and that they were no longer four sizes too big for the rest of her. Andy thought Donna was beautiful and from the number of boyfriends she had dated before Mike came along so did a lot of guys. Donna was very aware of her appearance and spent hours before a date fixing her hair and making sure her clothes were pressed just right.

One of Andy's favorite stories about Donna, the one he heard when he was hiding in his secret place behind the sofa listening to the adults talk, was about when she had taken on the town bully in a boxing match.

One summer when she was ten or eleven years old Ned got a set of boxing gloves for his birthday, and he and Donna were having a friendly sparring match in the backyard when a group of boys including Morris Metcalf, the large overweight loudmouth from up the street, stopped to watch the action. Morris began taunting her about how she fought like a girl and how ridiculous she looked. It made her angry. She told him to put up or shut up and invited him to put on the gloves. Ned told her she was crazy but agreed to let them go a few rounds.

Just as the first round began her father came from the barnyard and stood watching with the crowd of boys. For the first few minutes Morris kept Donna at bay with a series of jabs to her chin. All the while he grinned at her. Donna got more and more angry. Then Morris nailed her with a right cross and knocked her flat on her back. She was unhurt but began to cry and Morris made his first big mistake, he started to laugh. Donna, sobbing, ran to her dad who asked if she was hurt. She shook her head. He wiped her eyes, told her to watch out for the left jab, hit Morris in the stomach and pushed her back into the fray. Her face was getting red from the punches but she plunged back into the match.

Morris managed to keep her away for a minute with a couple more jabs, but then Donna got her first good punch to Morris' flabby stomach. The expression on his face changed dramatically and so did the momentum of the fight. After three hard punches to the retreating Morris' stomach, Donna changed her tactics and caught him on the side of the head with a roundhouse right that came up from her toes. Morris went down like a brick.

Dad went to Morris, helped him up and asked if he was all right. Morris made his second mistake, he said yes, so Dad pushed him back into the match. Morris was a little reluctant, but he went back to the fight.

The next three minutes were devastating for Morris. All he could do was try to throw jabs to protect himself, but Donna swarmed over him with a barrage of punches. Morris went down again, and again Dad helped him up.

"When you've had enough, just say so," Dad said, "and we'll declare Donna the winner and stop the fight."

Morris didn't want the boys to see him lose to a girl so he refused to quit. He lasted another minute before a straight right to his nose brought blood and knocked him down. When Dad pulled him to his feet, Morris said quietly he'd had enough.

Donna, face bright red from the punches and her eye puffy and watering, but with a grin from ear to ear, was declared the winner as the crowd cheered from the sideline.

Poor Morris. He never lived down the defeat and for the next few years he became the object of torment by the other kids who had suffered from his bullying.

One day later that summer Donna and two of her girlfriends ambushed Morris on his way home from school. They pinned him to the ground and threatened to de-pants him, but settled for hanging him by his feet. They couldn't lift him, he was too heavy; but they got his legs and butt far enough off the ground to wedge the heels of his high-topped shoes between the pickets and the top rail of the fence in front of his house. He couldn't get his heels free, but while he could lift himself high enough to untie his shoes, he couldn't get them off. The girls had escaped by the time his mother heard him yelling and came out to free him.

Andy laughed so hard at the story he was afraid the adults would discover him in his hiding place, but they too were laughing and he was not found out.

Sometimes his mother wouldn't bake one of the loaves of bread and would make flapjacks for supper. Ray's mother called them scones, but Andy's family always called them flapjacks. They were just chunks of bread dough fried in grease, sort of like lumpy golden pancakes, but they tasted different than regular bread. They were hot and light and when covered with butter and jam or honey they were delicious.

"Will you make some flapjacks for supper?" Andy yelled from his bed.

"Andrew, why didn't you ask me earlier?" Emma said coming to the doorway, "I only have enough dough for three loaves and you know your grandpa is coming tonight for the weekend. We'll need all three loaves. Maybe I'll do it tomorrow."

He sure would have liked some flapjacks, but when Mom called him Andrew he knew not to ask again.

Andy was staying in grandpa's bed. When his mom and dad bought the family farm from grandpa, he asked to have two rooms on the main floor of the house as an apartment. It was a place to keep some personal belongings and a place to stay when he came to town to visit his kids. When he was not in town and a family member got sick, they were put in grandpa's bedroom. The family didn't call it grandpa's place anymore they called it the sick room.

The room was used because it was on the ground floor so that Andy's mother didn't have to go up and down stairs, and because it was next door to the bathroom. There was no upstairs bathroom.

Andy wondered where grandpa would sleep this weekend. They didn't know he was coming when they put Andy in his bed.

Grandpa was pretty old. He got real sick quite a few years ago and had to quit farming. After he sold the farm to Dad, he sat around for about a year. Then he said he was bored and had to find something to do or go crazy so he moved to a city fifty miles away and got a job as a janitor. He had been there for as long as Andy could remember.

Those flapjacks would sure have tasted good. He could almost smell them. Wait a minute; he could smell them! Mom had saved enough dough for a couple of flapjacks for him, and she was frying them.

The sickroom was on the west front corner of the house and had two windows. From the west window Andy could watch the sunset and out the north window he could look down the street and see Ray's front yard.

Ray was a year ahead of Andy in school but they were only four months apart in age. Andy's birthday was in December and his parents were given the choice of letting him start school early or keep him out until the following year. Andy was small for his age so his parents decided to wait until the next year.

They didn't do it because he wasn't smart. He was as smart as anybody. He'd known his ABC's forward and backward since he was four years old. Aunt Ida taught him his ABC's backwards one day when she was tending him and he never forgot them. It was all in the rhythm.

Andy could print the alphabet long before he started school, and when he was five Donna taught him to write in script. Back when Donna was still in high school and Mike was away to college, she helped

Andy practice writing in script by letting him write letters to Mike for her. While she ironed or did other housework, Andy would sit at the kitchen table and as she spelled out the words he wrote them down.

Andy told his parents he wanted to go to school with Ray, but they thought it best to keep him out until the following year. All it did was cause problems for Andy. He was put with the younger group in school and with the older group in Sunday school and the Boy Scout troop. He didn't know where he belonged.

Andy could also see the old man's yard through the north window. The old man's name was Charlie. Andy knew that from hearing his parents talk, but all the kids just called him the old man. Andy was actually related to Charlie. Andy's grandmother on his mother's side and Charlie's dead wife were sisters, so old Charlie was his great-uncle by marriage. That was weird, but what was even weirder was that his mother's sister was his father's aunt. Dad's uncle, who was a couple of years older than him, married Andy's mother's older sister and that made Andy's aunt also his great aunt. It was weird and it made his head hurt.

Andy was ashamed of what happened at Charlie's house after he fell. Everyone said it was because he was delirious but Andy knew better, and he knew from the look in the old man's eyes when he was screaming that Charlie knew better too. He was scared, scared as hell. How could he have acted like that? It was the old man who found him on the sidewalk, took him in, called for his mother and cared for him; and all Andy did was scream.

His mother came into the room with two flapjacks on a tray.

"Here you go," she said. "I hope I can get the frying smell out of the house before the others get home. If they smell them they will all want flapjacks." She sat the tray next to Andy and went back to finish baking.

Ray, Johnny and Bobby, three of his friends and classmates, walked down the middle of the road on their way home from playing, probably out by the old canal. Bobby and Johnny lived further up the street so they must be going to Ray's house. Andy rapped on the window and waved.

They waved back. They came to see him after his fall, but he wasn't in the mood to talk. Now he felt better but nobody seemed to want to see him. All they probably wanted was to see how badly he got banged up in the fall. To hell with them, he didn't care.

The boys passed and Andy saw Charlie pulling his iron-wheeled milkcan cart up the path toward the front gate to pick up the cans. Every day the milk truck came by and picked up the full cans from all of the farmers in town, including Dad; and in the afternoon the clean, empty cans were dropped off at the pickup location. Not all cans were delivered to the stands in front of the house. Most farmers' milk cans were picked up from the cooling troughs in the barnyard and the empty cans returned next to the barn, but the lane to Charlie's barnyard didn't go all the way through the block because old man Grant wouldn't give the right of way for the lane. Because the milk truck couldn't turn around in Charlie's barnyard and couldn't back the half block down the lane to the street, he, like several other farmers around town, had his milk cans delivered to the stand in front of his house. It was extra work for those farmers with milk can stands but it was the only solution.

Charlie slowly opened the gate and pulled the cart through. He was really old. Mother said he was at least seventy-five, but he kept farming.

Andy's grandpa quit farming when he was in his early sixties and moved to the city. He wished he could spend more time with Grandpa. The other kids always talked about the great times they had with their grandmas and grandpas but Andy couldn't. Grandpa didn't visit often and all other grandparents had been dead for years.

Ray was lucky enough to have his great grandmother living with his family. She was a really great old lady. She was about Andy's age when she came across the plains with the pioneers. She told wonderful stories, although she did ramble a bit and Andy had to damn near yell to make her hear him; but he supposed that was to be expected from a women who was in her nineties.

Charlie loaded the milk cans in his cart and dragged the cart toward the barnyard. He didn't look at all scary now. He didn't seem to notice

Andy's friends when they went by. In fact, except the day Andy fell, the only time he had seen Charlie look at anything except the ground was when he stared at Andy from the barn window.

Andy felt awful about screaming when the old man was only trying to help him, and he wanted to tell him that he was sorry. His mother said he should forget it because Charlie understood he was delirious, but it still bothered Andy.

Andy was very young the first time he remembered seeing him, but the image stuck in his mind. Charlie was walking up the street. He was hunched over as if he couldn't hold up the massive weight of his shoulders. The cuffs of his faded blue bib overalls dragged on the sidewalk and stirred up a trail of dust as he trudged up the street. An old felt hat was pulled down over his eyes and he stared at the ground immediately in front of him, but the odd thing was that he carried a woman's purse over his arm. Andy watched him until he disappeared behind the row of poplar tree trunks.

Andy asked his mother why Charlie carried a purse, and she said his wife made him. His wife Bessie would call the market on the telephone and price each item she wanted to buy. She would make a list for him to give to the grocer and put the exact change in her purse and make him carry it to the grocery store. Andy couldn't understand why Charlie would do it, but he understood why the old man looked at the ground. He was embarrassed and Andy was embarrassed for him.

Charlie trudged down the path with his cart and the sound of the empty milk cans banging together faded behind the house.

Grandpa stayed an extra day to celebrate Memorial Day because it fell on Monday. He spent all afternoon with Andy's mother and father visiting the family graves. Andy was again disappointed that he didn't get to spend time with him. Andy really liked the stories Grandpa use to tell about the old days when he was growing up. It seemed like years since they spent time together and Andy missed it.

Andy didn't like Memorial Day. He thought it was weird to put flowers on dead people's graves. He never thought much about death or the dead, but his mother said it would be different someday when someone close to him passed over.

Passed over? That's sure a weird way to talk about being dead. Over where?

The only person he knew who died was the boy from across town who fell off a tractor and was run over. Andy hadn't known him very well because he was three years older and they never played together, but he did remember how bad everyone felt when it happened.

Three days in bed seemed like forever. Andy slept a lot during the day so he found himself awake at odd times. Sometimes he was awake for what seemed like hours in the middle of the night. If he were asleep, his father preparing to do morning chores would wake him at five in the morning. For two mornings he lay awake watching dawn break. He saw the lights go on in the old man's house and in a few minutes go out again and then Charlie would trudge down the path toward the barn.

He wondered what Charlie was like and what he thought about. Andy didn't wonder much about what people thought about, but Charlie was different because he never talked to anyone. He never went anywhere and he never had company. Ever since his wife died he had been alone, and that was longer than Andy could remember. He must be very lonely.

Andy's interest in the old man increased during the holiday weekend, when a lot of his parents' friends came to visit while they were in town to put flowers on family graves. When they heard about Andy's accident and how Charlie helped they invariably told some funny story about him; but the stories were never really about Charlie they were about his dead wife. Every story was about what a strange and terrible woman she was. Andy listened from his bed to the stories and, although the storytellers laughed, Andy didn't think the stories were funny. They were sad and made him wonder how Charlie could have stayed married for so long to such an awful woman.

Bessie was bossy, not only with Charlie but with everyone. She was so demanding people avoided her. Aunt Muriel told of the time years earlier when Bessie and a neighbor who lived down the street shared the cost for a set of curtain stretchers. Bessie demanded they be kept in her house, and when the neighbor wanted to use them they were given grudgingly. If they were not returned the next day she would march down the street and demand the return of "her" curtain stretchers. It became such a source of tension between them that the neighbor gave up her share and bought a set of her own. Bessie never mentioned them again nor did she offer to pay the neighbor for her half of the cost.

Mrs. West from up the street told how Bessie made Charlie stay in his corner of the house. Of course it was in the kitchen where the linoleum could be easily cleaned should he happen to track in mud on her spotless floor. Under his rocking chair and for three feet around she carefully taped newspapers to the floor. On one side of the chair was a small table on which she placed a bible. On the other side was a magazine rack filled with assorted newspapers and a number of magazines that most of the farmers received from seed and fertilizer companies.

He lived with her for more than forty years and to Mrs. West's knowledge he was never allowed to use the indoor bathroom. Even on freezing winter days Charlie trudged down the path to the outhouse by the barnyard gate.

Directly behind the house, a few steps from the back door was a coal shed and attached to the side of the shed was a shelf with a basin. A faucet came out from the foundation of the house next to the shed and attached to it was a short piece of garden hose. On one of the pegs on the inside of the shed door hung a towel and on the other a flannel shirt. After finishing the morning or evening chores Charlie washed his hands and face and changed his shirt before going into her house. Mrs. West heard a rumor that he was served his meals on the small table next to his chair. Andy wondered where he took a bath.

Andy heard the rattle of milk cans. Charlie brought the full cans in his cart and put them on the milk can stand.

Why hadn't Andy thought of it before? It was the perfect way to do something for the old man and solve his summer job problem at the same time. Andy would ask Charlie to let him drive his herd of cows for the summer. Nobody had ever driven his herd but Andy would ask. The herd had to be driven at least two miles west of town all the way down to the train tracks on the airport road. That was the same route Dad's herd took to their pasture. He could drive both herds.

When Andy was allowed out of bed and out of the house, he and Ray went out by the canal to play. It was still too cold to go swimming in the canal and his mother said that was out of the question anyway so they decided to make toy boats and have sailing races.

"I need to ask you something," Andy said.

"What?"

"I'm going to asked old Charlie if I can drive his herd this summer."

"You're crazy. Nobody has ever driven his cows because everybody is afraid of him," Ray said. "He's scary. I wouldn't go near him."

"I'm not scared," Andy said, but he knew it was a lie. "Because Ned's in the Army, I need to drive our herd this summer so, if I'm going to make some money, I've got to find a herd that goes to a pasture by my dad's. Charlie's pasture is just up the road from Dad's."

"I still think you're crazy," Ray said. "Besides, what makes you think the old man will let you drive for him?"

Andy shrugged. "Well, it won't hurt to ask."

Ray laughed.

"Since I have to drive our herd, that means I can't drive Uncle Jed's cows. What I needed to ask you is if you wanted the job. Do you?"

"Yeah, your Uncle Jed's pasture is just down the road from my other herd, and the corrals are on the same street. That's a great idea. Thanks."

Andy swore Ray to secrecy. He didn't want anyone to know his plan until he had the job. Ray said he still thought Andy was crazy to go near the old man, but he agreed not to tell anyone. Andy hoped he had the courage to act on his plan.

Mom didn't want him playing at the trash dump. She was afraid Andy would catch some dreaded disease or cut himself and get blood poisoning. There wasn't much else to do, so in spite of his mother's warning he went with Ray and Johnny to the trash dump east of town to search for treasure.

They spent a couple of hours rummaging through the discarded boxes. A "find" had to be pretty special for Andy to take it home because if he kept something his mother would know that he had been playing at the dump and he'd catch all kinds of hell.

Today wasn't his day. Ray found a great old beaver hat and a pair of suspenders, but Andy found nothing worth the hassle he'd have to face if he kept something.

On the way home they took turns kicking a tin can down the street. Each tried to out-distance the previous kick. You scored points for distance, but also for keeping the can on the straight course down the middle of the road.

Andy saw Charlie with his milk cart in front of his house picking up the empty cans. Ray and Johnny joked about how odd the old man was and how funny he looked. Andy knew Charlie could hear them even though he didn't look up from his task. Andy felt flushed as the blood rushed to his face. He was embarrassed, said he had to go and ran home.

After chores Andy was on the front porch lounging in the swing, waiting. He decided tonight was the night he would ask the old man if he could drive his cows. If he didn't do it soon it would be too late.

He waited in the swing until he saw Charlie turning his cows out of the barn into the corral for the night. Then Andy ran across the street. From the front gate he saw Charlie come out of the barn and close the door. Slowly, his heart pounding, he walked down the path to meet the old man. It was the first time he had been in Charlie's yard, the only time he remembered anyway. Andy stopped by the coal shed and waited when he came through the barnyard gate. The old man raised his head slightly and then lowered it as he came up the path. He was looking at his hands as he took off his leather gloves. His hands were very rough and Andy thought they looked as much like leather as the gloves. Andy's heart pounded and his mouth was dry. He licked his lips and tried to swallow but the lump stayed in his throat. He tried to clear his throat as the old man approached. Charlie took no notice of the boy. He brushed past him and went into the shed. Andy didn't know what to do. He wanted to run but stood his ground. It seemed like he waited forever. Finally the shed door opened and Charlie came out. He had changed his shirt. He went directly to the faucet, filled the basin with water and began washing his hands and face. Andy wasn't afraid anymore, but he didn't know what to say. Charlie finished washing and dried his hands and face on the towel.

"Can I drive your cows to pasture this summer?" Andy almost shouted.

The old man shrugged his shoulders. Andy didn't know if he meant yes or no.

"I've been driving cows for three years," he went on. He was talking too loud and too fast, but he was nervous and it was either keep talking or run. "Last year I drove cows for Uncle Jed." That was a dumb thing to say. The old man knew that. Andy felt stupid and he felt the blood rising in his face. "I mean you can ask him if I did a good job," Andy said, "I always got the cows home on time."

The old man started for the kitchen door, but Andy had his courage up so he followed. As Charlie climbed the three steps to the back door he turned and said, "Okay."

"How much?" Andy asked quickly.

The old man shrugged his shoulders.

"I figure it's about two miles to your pasture, and with the number of cows you've got I thought maybe four dollars a month."

The old man did not move.

"If that's too much, I'll do it for three."

"Four's okay," the old man said. It was almost inaudible. His voice was deep, calm and without emotion. It was not the voice Andy imagined he would have. It was not gravelly or gruff.

Andy smiled. "When do you want me to start?"

"Monday."

"What time?"

"Seven thirty," the old man said and went into the house.

"Thanks," Andy yelled as he ran up the walk to the front gate. He closed the gate and put the metal hoop over the gatepost. The old man was standing in the doorway. Andy waved and the old man stepped back and closed the door.

Andy ran across the street smiling. He'd done it. He'd talked to the old man. He plopped down on the porch swing. The lights in old Charlie's house were on and Andy could see him through the living room window shuffling back and forth in the kitchen with a pan in his hand. Andy watched him until he moved out of sight and didn't reappear.

The sun was setting behind the rugged mountains to the west, and without light shining on the face of the mountains they appeared to be flat, like an enormous pale blue cardboard cutout. They looked unreal.

The yard and street were streaked with the elongated shadows cast by the poplar trees. The amber rays of evening light illuminated the dust in the air and Andy could see the beams of light. They reminded him of his illustrated book of Bible stories. In the pictures the shafts of light streamed down on the prophets when they talked with God.

Andy liked this time of day. The long shadows, the golden light that made everything look so warm and glowing, the stillness of the valley air before the canyon breeze starts rustling through the poplars, all these things together made this time of day peaceful and inviting. It would be a warm night and Andy decided he would sleep outside, something he did most summer nights. He wouldn't invite Ray over tonight. He wanted to lie by himself and look at the stars.

The light went out in Charlie's kitchen. Andy wondered what he was doing. It was much too early to go to bed. Was he sitting in that dark house looking out at him? Andy got the same feeling he did when he saw the old man staring at him from the barn window. A chill shot up his spine and he ran into the house.

Maybe it's not such a good idea to drive cows for the old man, Andy thought.

Suddenly Andy realized he hadn't asked Dad for permission to drive Charlie's herd.

Oh hell!

With a lot of apprehension he went into the kitchen where his mom and dad were sitting at the table talking. He told them what he had done, and to his surprise his mother seemed quite pleased that he was going to drive cows for Charlie. Dad said it was all right with him. He needed Andy to drive his herd, and because of the closeness of Charlie's pasture Andy could drive both herds. Andy looked for some sign between his parents, some look between them, some sound or word to tell him he shouldn't do it, but there was none.

Dad said he would drive his herd for the first week until the cows got used to going to pasture. Once they were in their routine it would be easy for Andy to drive both herds together. He could get Charlie's herd headed down the street and open the corral and get Dad's herd as they passed. The two herds would separate when they got to their pasture. The old man's herd would go into their pasture and his dad's herd would continue down the road to their pasture. Andy didn't know how or why they would do it, but he knew they would.

Everything seemed to be working out perfectly, but Andy was still a little apprehensive about being around the old man.

The next evening when they were finishing the chores, Andy told Dad that he didn't know if he'd done the right thing when he asked Charlie if he could drive his herd.

"I'm kind of scared of him," he said. "He acts so strange."

"You might be afraid of him now, but when you get to know him he's a pretty nice old guy," Dad said.

"You know him?" Andy asked. "I've never seen you talk to him. I thought you were scared of him too."

"No Andy, I'm not scared of him. I used to talk to him all the time, but after his wife died he changed. He was never very talkative, and he got even quieter after she was gone. He just stopped being around people. I imagine he's pretty lonely. I'll bet he might like to have somebody to talk to."

"You mean I should talk to him?"

"It wouldn't hurt to try."

"What would we talk about?" Andy asked.

"You're always saying how much you miss your grandpa and the stories he used to tell you," Dad said. "Well, Charlie's older than your grandpa so I'll bet he knows a lot of stories about the old days."

What Dad said intrigued Andy, but he was still a bit scared.

IV

Charlie sat in his rocking chair looking out the kitchen window. He had washed the supper dishes. The eggs he boiled were too hard. He hadn't paid attention to the time again and overcooked them. They looked kind of green but he ate them. He could have cooked more but it wasn't important. Eggs are eggs. He learned long ago it was easier to eat what was put in front of you than complain. Bessie was never a very good cook.

Why had the boy asked to drive his cows? No one had ever asked before. His parents probably suggested it as a way to repay him for helping the boy. They probably felt sorry for him. He didn't want anyone feeling sorry for him. Maybe he should tell the boy he didn't need any help, but he did; and it would be very nice not to have to walk to the pasture and back twice every day. Besides, he could really use the extra time in the fields; and four dollars was reasonable. He decided he would let the boy take the cows to pasture and see what happened.

He shifted in his chair and the newspapers under the rockers tore from the sliding. He got up and went to the counter by the stove for new tape and newspapers. He passed the door to the living room and through the front window he saw the boy run into the house. He replaced the papers, opened the kitchen door and sat down heavily in his chair. It would be another evening of nothing.

Outside, the crickets joined in the building symphony of night sounds. The canyon breeze rustled the poplar leaves. He wished Bessie were here, although she wasn't very good company, especially after things changed in their marriage. Usually all she did was sit and sew some flowery pattern on a dishtowel or complain that he hadn't fixed something she thought needed to be repaired before the entire house collapsed around them, but she had been there.

After the first few years there was never much love in their marriage. Bessie felt trapped because she hadn't had a chance to see the world. She changed so much during the more than forty-five years they were together. When their courtship began Bessie had fine golden corn-silk hair. She became self-conscious when it started thinning and white replaced the yellow. She never changed her hairstyle after 1920 because she thought the close-set waves hid the pink scalp that was apparent on the crown of her head. He never noticed until she pointed it out to him.

When she was young Bessie was pretty. Charlie thought she was delicate and vulnerable; that too changed.

During their courtship they went on wonderful carriage rides and picnics. He remembered the ribbing he got from the other boys when he announced in Sunday school that he was going to marry Bessie. He had known that he was going to marry her long before he announced it to his classmates. His deep-set eyes filled with tears and he wiped them away with his sleeve. Considering everything, it had been a good life. Bessie was difficult at times and he knew other people did not take to her, but she was his wife.

When did Bessie change? There was a time when she was always smiling and very charming, but Charlie remembered that the changes began a couple of years after they were married. Both of them wanted to have a family, but try as she did to get with child, it didn't happen. Bessie sought help from their doctor and was told that there was something wrong, Charlie didn't know what because she wouldn't tell him. The Doctor said that she would most likely never have a child. Bessie seemed to take the news well. She said they could have a full life without children.

Charlie was really shaken because he wanted a son very much. He wanted a boy to teach and give all the things he felt he had missed in life. He wanted to take his son fishing and teach him how to plow and irrigate the fields. Bessie helped him accept things as they were.

He was never one to go to church. Bessie was the one who went to church. Soon after they learned they would have no children Bessie stopped going too. At first she would say she didn't feel well, then she said she was too busy preparing Sunday dinner; and then she simply said she didn't want to go anymore.

A local farmer had eleven children and not enough room to house them or enough money to provide for them so three of his older boys were going to move in with neighbors and help them on their farms in return for room and board. Charlie wanted to take in one of the boys, but Bessie would not hear of it. She said she wouldn't raise a child that was not her own.

Somehow Bessie got the idea that people were talking about her behind her back. He told her people didn't talk about them and that people understood it was no one's fault they couldn't have children, but she would not listen. She was certain they were talking about her and making fun of her.

She started criticizing the town and the people. She wanted to leave and move to the city. He couldn't do that. He owed too much on the farm and didn't have the skills to get a job in the city. They fought about it for years and then the depression hit and they couldn't leave. There were no jobs to be had and they couldn't get anything from selling the farm so they stayed. They stopped fighting or even talking about it, but Bessie got worse. He tried to help by not upsetting her and doing everything she asked to have done. It got worse. She didn't trust the townspeople. She didn't go out into the community and they lived their lives in silence. What little conversation they had was about the daily routine. They never dreamed or planned for the future. Charlie didn't like to think about those days.

He had never thought of life without Bessie until one morning she was gone.

Charlie had been making his way from the barnyard up the path toward the house pulling the iron-wheeled milk cart. The train going south down by the airport road let out a shrill whistle at the old river road crossing. The screech pierced the cold autumn air. It sounded like the train was just down the street. Charlie, deep in thought, was startled by the sound, and then he noticed something was different. There were no lights in the kitchen window. The porch light he turned on before going to milk the cows was still burning and there was no smoke spiraling from the chimney. He froze in his tracks. She always, as was her frugal nature, turned the porch light off before beginning the daily routine of preparing breakfast. He let the cart drop and the two full milk cans clanged together as they slid to the front of the cart. He walked, slowly at first, then faster and faster toward the back door. When he opened the door there were no sounds, no smells of breakfast and no warmth in the air.

"Bessie," he almost whispered and then again louder he called her name.

He was three steps inside the house when he remembered he still had on his chore clothes and dirty boots. He hesitated, almost turned to go out and change but caught himself, turned and went to the bedroom door. Almost leaning against the doorframe he slowly pushed the door open quietly so as not to wake her. She was lying in bed, the pink and white patchwork quilt neatly tucked around her shoulders. Charlie walked to the bed and gently put the back of his huge hand to her neck, and the memory of the touch of her skin, avoided for so long, flowed through him. Her skin was still as soft as ever but it was cold. His body stiffened and his big hand fell to his side.

"Oh Bessie," he said.

Emma Parker was cooking a pot of oatmeal when Charlie appeared at the backdoor. The knock startled her because it was too early for anyone to be about and Emma was lost in thought. Morning was her time. She enjoyed the hour of calm and quiet before her husband and son came in from chores and the other children got up. It was her time to dream. She moved the oatmeal to the back of the wood burning stove and opened the door.

"Bessie's dead. Can you help please?" Charlie said softly. Then he slowly shuffled back across the street.

When the Parkers knocked on his back door there was no response so they opened it and went inside. Charlie was sitting in his rocking chair. He had changed into his house clothes and was slowly rocking back and forth. He did not stop rocking or look up when they entered.

The next few days were a frenzy of activity with the funeral arrangements and all, but Charlie never said a word. The only response he made during those emotional days was to nod. Relatives made the decisions and arrangements. Those who were not angry with Charlie were concerned about him, but they could do nothing.

At the usual time morning and evening Charlie would rise from his chair, go to the shed by the back porch, put on his chore clothes, do the chores, milk the cows and perform the other duties that were his daily routine. The doctor told relatives there was nothing medically wrong with him, and there was no reason to put him in the hospital. He ate and functioned but did not connect with others. There was little anyone could do for him. There was nothing to do but wait and see if he came around.

Winter passed without Charlie speaking to anyone. The neighbor ladies saw to it that the house was kept clean, but it was Charlie who, after they had gone, would tape the newspapers under his rocking chair. The women found there was really little to do since he rarely used any of the rooms other than the kitchen and his bedroom. He was seen from time to time trudging down the path to the outhouse by the barnyard gate.

He continued to carry the purse when he went to the market. He would gather the items he needed, always the same, and count out the exact change to the storekeeper without saying a word. It was as if she had not died. There was talk around town that he had lost his senses and should be put in a home.

Charlie knew why he didn't speak. Even though their life together was anything but happy, she was all he had. He was so devastated by the loss of Bessie that he didn't dare speak for fear he would break into tears. He couldn't let people see him cry. He couldn't show them how weak he really was, so he said nothing.

It was well into spring when he finally got his emotions under control. He hated that the neighborhood women were constantly around trying to do something for him. He didn't need anything, and he didn't want their help, so when he finally spoke it was to tell them to mind their own business. They did exactly that, and it had been years since anyone visited him. The townspeople accepted his odd behavior and soon settled back to their routine and he was left alone.

Charlie thought that was fine. He was never much of a talker anyway. As a boy he found it difficult to speak up in a group, and things didn't get any easier for him as he grew older. Perhaps that was why his announcement that he was going to marry Bessie came as such a surprise to his peers.

Bessie and Charlie were married in spring of the year he turned twenty-one, and it was two years later to the day when he finished building the house.

The farm they bought was one of the oldest in town. Along with the farmyard and house in town, the farm consisted of three parcels of arable land north, south and east of town for crops and a pasture west of town. There was a good barn and outbuildings, and the corral fence had just been rebuilt when the man who owned the place died. His widow couldn't run it so she sold it to Charlie and Bessie. The problem they faced was that the house was really a cabin, and a very old cabin at that. It had two rooms with only a cold-water faucet in the kitchen and no indoor plumbing. The outhouse was down by the barnyard gate.

Charlie had to build a new house. They lived in the cabin for two years while he built the new house in the calf pasture west of the cabin. When the house was finished, he tore down the cabin and that area would later become the calf pasture.

It was difficult for him to run the farm by day and build at night, but he didn't have the money after making the down payment on the farm to hire someone to help him build. It was especially difficult for Bessie to live in the rustic cabin with no plumbing.

They moved into their home right after the town council made the decision to beautify the streets by planting poplar trees. The young trees were brought around on Joe Waite's flatbed wagon, and each homeowner was given enough trees to plant them twenty-five feet apart across the front of their yard. They were to be planted on the city-owned strip of land between the sidewalk and the road.

Bessie was delighted and eager to help him plant the seedlings. She said she could hardly wait for them to grow large enough to provide some shady relief from the sun beating on the south side of the house. To keep the interior somewhat cool until the trees grew Charlie made slat awnings for the south and west windows of the house. It seemed like such a short time before he was taking them down. The poplars grew quickly and within a few years the town seemed cooler and the streets looked lush and inviting.

Now Bessie was gone and all but two of the five trees were gone too. The trees were blown over by the spring winds two years ago. One crushed two sections of the picket fence and narrowly missed the porch on the southeast corner of the house. It took him weeks to clear the debris. He wanted help but he asked no one, and no one volunteered.

For two years the summer sun again beat on the living room windows. The room was stifling so he spent his evenings in the kitchen or on the bench by the coal shed.

Charlie hadn't thought about his life with Bessie for a long time, and he wondered why he was thinking of her tonight.

Despite having the kitchen door open, the early summer heat building in the living room was drifting into the kitchen. Charlie went into the living room and opened the side windows and his bedroom window before escaping to the bench to wait for the evening breeze to cool the sweltering house so that he could sleep. Another summer of heat, and another evening of nothing.

V

Monday morning Andy with his bicycle arrived at the gate of Charlie's corral at exactly seven-thirty. The cows were in the corral, the barn was locked and Charlie was nowhere in sight. Andy thought it would be a good idea to go to the house and get the old man to help him with the herd because this was their first morning to go to pasture. He knew that every year until the cows got used to going to pasture they would be so anxious to get at the fresh grass after eating dry hay all winter that they often ran all the way to the pasture. It wouldn't be a problem unless there were new cows in the herd. If one of the old man's heifers had a calf she would be in the herd, but she probably wouldn't have been to the pasture and she might be a problem. If the old man bought a cow over the winter and Andy let her out of the corral she might just go to her old pasture. Once a cow breaks from the herd strange things happen. He might have cows going in all directions. The old man knew what time Andy would arrive, and he knew the problems with driving cows to pasture the first time in spring, so if he wasn't around Andy had to assume all the cows had been to pasture the previous year.

Andy had another problem. He was unfamiliar with the herd. He hadn't been around them enough to identify them. The cows were all Holsteins and some had very distinct markings he could easily recognize, but some looked pretty much alike. If he lost one of those, Andy might have a difficult time finding her.

With some apprehension Andy unlatched the gate, swung it wide open and went into the corral. The cows eyed him curiously as he moved toward them. Some were lying down chewing their cuds after their morning grain ration. When he got them to their feet and moved the herd toward the open gate a change came over the herd. Suddenly the cows streamed toward the gate and as Andy ran to the corner of the corral to get the last and laziest cow to her feet—there is always one in every herd—he saw over his shoulder that most of the herd was running down the lane toward the street. Old cows with sagging udders and not enough energy to get out of his way a minute earlier were kicking up their heels and bouncing down the lane like yearling heifers. Once they reached the street they went in all directions.

Andy didn't get the cows in the pasture until nine-thirty. When he finally got the two that went north headed in the right direction, the remainder of the herd that went south were nowhere in sight. He decided, after almost giving up on the whole thing, to take the two cows he had under control to the pasture and search for the others later. He hoped at least some of the old cows would be in the pasture. He arrived at the pasture with the two cows just in time to overtake the old cow he herded out of the corral last as she slowly ambled through the pasture gate. He counted the cows already in the pasture. One was missing, and he didn't know which one it was. They had all headed south when he went after the two strays. Somewhere between the main road where they turned west and the pasture was a cow, and he didn't know what she looked like. There was nothing to do but try to find her. He started backtracking on his bicycle. He checked all of the lanes on both sides of the road, and he made sure there were no cows in the fields with open gates.

Cows seemed to remember where their pasture was from year to year. Everyone said cows were stupid and Andy agreed, but somehow they always seemed to know how to get to their pasture. Andy hoped the old man hadn't bought his missing cow from someone who lived in the next town. That would be where his lost cow would be heading, and he might never find her.

Andy retraced his route almost back to town and found nothing except one mangy yearling steer outside the Davenport place. It was obviously one of those animals that spent all of its time at the fence line trying to get through to the grass on the other side, and once through the fence it decides that it wants to be back inside so it wanders the fence line looking for a way back.

The only thing left to do was to try to find out in what field the old man was working and go and ask where he got the animal. Then he would go to the pasture of the former owner and see if the cow was there.

As he turned off the main road toward Charlie's house he saw Mr. Otis, another of the town's older farmers, driving a single cow his way. It could be the lost cow.

"Is that old Charlie's cow, Mr. Otis?" Andy asked as he pulled his bike alongside the farmer's horse.

"Yep, I guess it got out and decided to come home." The old farmer chuckled. "They do that every so often you know."

"It didn't get out. I was driving his herd to pasture for the first time this spring and she sort of got away."

The old farmer laughed. "You drivin' Charlie's herd this year, Andy?"

"Yes."

"I don't recall anybody ever drivin' cows for Charlie," Mr. Otis said, "How come you're doin' it this year?"

"It's a pretty good herd and I just thought maybe he would like some help," Andy said.

The old farmer smiled. "It's about time someone took notice of Charlie. If I had any kids, I would have sent them around. Charlie's a good old fellow. I've known him for as long as I can remember. Just wish he wouldn't keep to himself so much. Not healthy. Your dad sent you over, huh?"

"No, it was my idea," Andy said. "Because Ned's in the Army, I've got to drive Dad's cows; and he said I could drive another herd if I could find one that went down by our pasture. Charlie's does so I thought I'd ask him."

"I'm glad you did," Mr. Otis said. "You know Charlie would give you the shirt off his back if you needed it. Why don't you ask him to show you his collection of arrowheads sometime? He's got a lot of them and some of them are damn good ones."

The cow was crossing the main road and heading back to the old man's corral. Andy pedaled his bike in front of her and headed her down the main road toward the pasture. When the cow was headed in the right direction Mr. Otis turned his horse and started for home.

"Thanks," Andy called, "and please don't tell anyone how I botched up the drive this morning."

The old farmer laughed, waved and spurred his horse into a gallop.

The cow wanted to stop in every open field and take every side road. Andy had to speed past her and cut her off many times. He knew she was going to be the cow to cause him trouble all summer.

What Mr. Otis said kept going through Andy's head. He never heard anyone speak of the old man as a friend, as a good old fellow; and he had a collection of arrowheads. There were a lot of things about Charlie Andy didn't know, but he also didn't know how to make friends with him either. The old man didn't seem to want to talk to him or be around him.

Mr. Otis was different. Andy really liked him. He became friends with the tall, angular old man when he used to hang out at the service station. Mr. Otis was about the only one of the group of adults who sat around the station gossiping who didn't seem to mind if Andy was there listening. It seemed to him that Mr. Otis liked talking to him as much as Andy enjoyed talking to Mr. Otis. He smiled and laughed a lot when they talked, and he was always friendly when he saw Andy at church or around town. Andy thought maybe it was because Mr. Otis and his wife never had any kids that he took the time to listen and be friendly with kids. All the kids liked him, and he never got pestered or teased by the older boys in town. If anyone ever tried he would probably just laugh and invite them into his house for a treat. Mr. Otis surely wouldn't go around telling everyone how badly Andy had screwed up his first day on the job.

The last cow safely in the pasture, Andy headed for home. The sun was already high and it was getting hot. He sure hoped Charlie wouldn't find out how long it took him to get the herd to pasture. Besides, by being so late he was in enough trouble with Dad for not being home and ready to go to the field with him.

The old man said nothing to him, and Dad actually laughed when Andy tried to explain what happened.

Despite his not too auspicious first day on the job, Andy had the cows settled into a routine within the week, when it was time to add Dad's herd to the drive. Everything went just as he knew it would. There were some antics on the way to the pastures as the cows did what they do to get to know other cows, but by the time the herds reached the pastures they separated and went into the right one. From now on the job would be a snap.

Why did anyone need to drive cows except for the first few days anyway? Cows are such creatures of habit. For the first few days Andy had to go to the back of the pasture to get some of the young cows, but by the fourth day the entire herd was waiting at the gate when he arrived at the pasture. In the morning he would open the gate and they would file out of the corral the same way they filed into the barn at milking time. If Andy found something interesting along the side of the road or in one of the streams that flowed near the road, he could stop and play for a while and the cows would calmly continue their trek to or from the pasture. Andy thought somebody should invent a device that would automatically open the corral gate at seven-thirty, close the pasture gate at eight, then open the pasture gate at five-thirty and close the corral gate at six. There would be no need for anyone to follow the cows after the first week. They knew where to go.

Saturday night Andy slept outside in the backyard with Ray. They played games, talked and kept from going to sleep until Dad yelled at them from the bedroom window that it was two o'clock and they had better damn well shut up and get to sleep.

When Andy awoke his sleeping bag was hot and he was sweating from the heat of the morning sun that was already high in the sky. He was late. It was past eight when he jumped up, dressed and woke up Ray who also had cows to take to pasture. What a day to be late, he thought. If it were any other day of the week Charlie would be in the fields and would not know, but this was the one day of the week he would be home. As Andy pedaled his bike up the lane toward the corral, he saw the old man by the watering trough.

Now I'm going to get it, Andy thought. He tried to think of a good excuse but nothing seemed believable. He would simply tell the old man the truth. *What's the difference if I'm a little late anyway?* Andy knew that was a stupid thought. Dad told him the reason lots of times. If you are late you are cutting down on the feeding time for the cows. The pastures west of town were good but not the best in the world, and the cows needed time to find the new grass.

The cows were all standing by the gate mooing up a storm. Andy got off his bike and opened the gate. The cows crowded past him and hurried down the lane. He saw that the old man was still by the trough and called to him. "I'm sorry I'm late. I overslept. It won't happen again." He jumped on his bike and headed down the lane after the cows. They were already halfway down the block.

He caught up with the cows and looked back over his shoulder to see what the old man was doing. He was still standing by the trough looking at Andy.

"Damn, he's probably really mad at me now," Andy said aloud, "I don't think he likes me very much. I'll probably never get to see that arrowhead collection."

VI

Charlie's knees hurt constantly. The rheumatism had grown progressively worse over the past few years. He often woke in the middle of the night in pain and was unable to go back to sleep. The pills he took didn't seem to help anymore. The only thing that eased the nagging pain was to get up and walk around for a while.

He sat in his chair slowly rocking back and forth. He had gotten out of bed and walked around the dark silent house from room to room for longer than usual, but tonight it didn't help. He decided to dress and go to the barnyard and push the hay the cows always pushed out of the manger back within their reach.

The summer night was warm. Charlie closed the kitchen door behind him and started down the path to the barnyard. Now that he had constant pain in his knees, he was thankful he didn't have to make the trek to and from the pasture each day. He was pleased the boy was driving his herd. He liked the boy. There was something almost familiar about him and Charlie wished he could see him more and perhaps get to know him, but cultivating the corn field and cleaning out the irrigation ditches took his time. He wasn't around when the boy came to take the cows or brought them home in the evening.

He wondered when and how the boy wanted to be paid. The boy had been working for almost two weeks. Was he expecting to be paid once a month or every two weeks? It was something the boy had not asked about and since no one had ever driven his cows he did not know how it should be done. Sunday he would see the boy when he came to take the cows and ask him.

The cool canyon breeze rustled in the poplars. In the moonlight he saw the new leaves shimmering silver against the deep blue sky. He loved to be out at night when he was young, especially in the mountains. There are more stars than one could ever imagine on a night like this.

In the distance, somewhere over by the Lambert place, a group of kids was playing a night game. He listened for a moment. The glow of their bonfire cast light on the trees out by the old canal, and he could hear the sounds of "Olly Olly Oxen Free." They still played the same games he played many years ago except he couldn't have played so late into the night. When he was a kid there was always a chance a group of renegade Indians might come around. It seemed very long ago and yet the sounds, the gaiety and laughter were so familiar it only seemed like yesterday.

He pushed the hay back into the manger with the broken-handled pitchfork and started back up the path. His life was empty. He wanted very much to do something to get some enjoyment from his remaining years, but there was no one and he didn't know how to change things. He went inside, undressed and went to bed.

Sunday morning after chores were finished he ate breakfast quickly while keeping an eye on the corral to make sure he did not miss the boy if he happened to come for the cows early. Just before seven-thirty he put on his hat and went to the corral. The boy did not come for the cows at the scheduled time so he waited, filling the time by cleaning out the moss that had built up in the watering trough. When the boy arrived he yelled something about being late and being sorry and was gone before Charlie could muster the courage to talk to him. He watched a few minutes until the boy and the herd turned the corner and moved out of sight and then he walked slowly up the path to the house.

Why hadn't he called after the boy? He would have to talk to him in the evening or wait until next Sunday. He would see the boy tonight when he brought the cows home.

Charlie sat in his chair watching through the open kitchen door as the midday shadows crept across the lawn. Time seemed to go very slowly and it bothered him. He had never been one to wait. He was always finding something to do to fill the time, but he was waiting, waiting for evening to talk to the boy. For the first time in years he really wanted to talk to someone. The wages for driving the cows was just an excuse. He smiled to himself. He liked the feeling, not the feeling of waiting but the feeling of wanting to talk. Why the boy? He had been and probably still was frightened of Charlie. He didn't want to cause problems.

After an afternoon of anticipation when the time was drawing near for the boy to bring the cows home, Charlie put two one dollar bills in an envelope and taped it to the latch on the corral gate. He did not go out again until the cows were home and mooing to be milked.

The following evening after supper Charlie went out to water his garden. His vegetable garden was just east and in back of the house, and for as long as he had planted a garden he'd gotten the irrigation water from the ditch that flowed down the street between the poplar trees and the road. The ditch in front of his house actually flowed through a culvert that went through the bottom of his milk can stand.

On every street in town an east-west ditch provided water for gardens and calf pastures. The ditches in the lower part of town were filled with water from a canal a block and a half up the street. The upper part of town had ditches that were fed by the upper canal. When there was enough water, the ditches ran constantly during the summer. Any water not used flowed back into a canal down the street or west of town. Everyone who owned water rights could divert part of the water from the ditch to irrigate their gardens and calf pastures. It didn't take more than an hour to water the garden, but it was a task that required constant attention if one didn't want to waste water, because the stream had to be changed from one set of rows to the next every fifteen minutes.

Long ago Charlie had built a small wooden dam-like structure across the ditch at the east end of his property. He had diverted water from the ditch to one that took it to his garden by placing boards in front of the dam. The higher he stacked the boards the more water was diverted. It usually only took two 2"x 6" boards to divert enough to water his garden.

Charlie got boards and his shovel from the shed and went to his dam. There was plenty of water in the ditch so two boards would be all he would need. He knelt to place the first board when he was startled.

"Hello Charlie."

He dropped the board and grabbed it to keep it from floating downstream.

"Did I scare you? Sorry about that. I thought you heard me coming," Mr. Otis said.

"Hello Bill. No I didn't hear your horse coming. Guess I wasn't paying attention," Charlie said. "Where are you headed?"

"Out to the north field. I've got water on the alfalfa that I've got to change," Mr. Otis said. "Oh, I hear Andy Parker is driving cows for you this summer. I don't know why you haven't had someone do it before now."

"I didn't know anybody to ask."

"Andy's a good kid. You'll like him."

"Do you know him?" Charlie asked.

"Sure. I talk to him all the time down at the service station," Mr. Otis said with a laugh. "I saw him the first day he took your cows to pasture. That day the heifer you traded me for that steer came home, and I helped him get her headed the right way." Then he remembered he told Andy he wouldn't tell about Andy's first day on the job.

"He didn't tell me that."

"And he won't," Mr. Otis said with a laugh. "I wasn't supposed to tell you about that. I told him I wouldn't so don't mention it to him, okay?"

Charlie nodded.

"By the way, have you ever talked to him to find out if he's had any problems?"

"No. I just thought if he had problems, he would tell me."

"Charlie, other than me and the grocer when was the last time you talked to anyone?"

"I don't know."

"Why don't you come down to the service station some evening and sit around with the guys? They still ask about you," Mr. Otis said. "You'd like it. It would get you back into doing things with other people."

"I can't."

"Why not?"

"By the time I finish chores and eat it's this time of night. The service station is closed by now ain't it?" Charlie said. "Besides, I'm too old and tired to walk down there."

"If you don't drive a car, why don't you get a horse?"

"I can't afford to feed one. If I could I'd have one," Charlie said. "Driving cows wouldn't be so tough on me if I had a horse."

"Well you need to be around more people. Maybe you should get to know Andy," Mr. Otis said. "He's a pretty good kid."

"Yeah, but I'm not sure what I'd say to him."

"Hell, I told him about your arrowhead collection and he got real excited."

Charlie smiled. "You remember my arrowhead collection?"

"It's a good one, Charlie, and all kids are interested in stuff like that. I know Andy is."

"If I get a chance, maybe I will," Charlie said.

"Well, I've got to go. I've got to get that water changed before dark," Mr. Otis said. "I'll see you again soon. Oh, and say hello to Andy for me."

Charlie watched Bill Otis ride off and then put the boards in the dam. It was well past dark by the time he finished irrigating.

He sat in his chair and looked across the street until the lights in the Parker house went out.

Charlie was beginning to realize just how alone he was and that he really missed other people.

Maybe I can get to know the boy. Maybe things can change, but I shouldn't get my hopes up.

VII

June passed. It was a good summer for Andy. He went fishing with his dad eleven times on the river in the canyon. When he wasn't working for Dad, he sometimes went down the road below the pasture a mile past the railroad tracks to where the stream went under the road and fished using a worm and bobber. By lying on the bridge on his stomach he fished under the bridge and caught sunfish, bluegill and catfish; but real fishing meant fishing on the river for trout. Fishing was Dad's favorite sport and he was very good at it. Andy wanted to be a great fly fisherman and he knew someday he would become one.

He also went swimming with Ray and Johnny when they didn't have to work. They swam in the old canal until the canal company put poison in the water to kill the moss. As a precaution the canal company warned the farmers to keep their cattle from drinking the water for a day. The poison wouldn't kill cattle but too much could make them sick. The company attached signs on posts along the canal bank warning the kids that they couldn't swim for a week after the water was poisoned.

Usually the kids didn't go swimming for a couple of weeks after the water had been poisoned because the swimming was awful. Every time you dove into the canal you would come to the surface with strands of dead moss hanging all over you. Even wading was terrible. If you stood in the water, dead moss washing down stream draped around your legs. It was slimy and felt like some weird boneless sea creature. Once they poisoned the canal water swimming was over until early September.

Preparations for Donna's wedding in August were progressing. Emma and Donna continued to sew most evenings. Andy thought

Donna had enough dishtowels and pillowcases to supply an army. Either she was planning to have a very large family or she never planned to sew again for the rest of her life.

Donna got letters from Mike at least once and sometimes twice a week. He was due to come home on furlough two days before the wedding. Donna said he was cutting it pretty close. If something unexpected happened and he was delayed it would sure mess up all the wedding plans, but if he were allowed to come home earlier they wouldn't have much time for their honeymoon trip. Donna was getting pretty nervous about the whole affair.

Andy's mother only got letters from Ned about every two or three weeks, and it was an occasion she waited for with great anticipation. The letter she received in mid-June made her cry, and she was worried and upset for weeks afterward. Dad told her there was nothing they could do so she might as well relax. Ned had just gotten out of the hospital with some disease. Mom worried because she didn't think Ned was telling her everything about his condition. Andy asked if it was the same sickness Ned had when he was home on furlough after basic training. Dad said it wasn't. What he had now he caught over there.

Andy idolized his brother Ned. He was much older than Andy, but they used to talk about and do all sorts of things. He liked it that Ned was patient with him when he made a mistake or was unable to do something on the first try. Ned always took care to show Andy how something was properly done and helped him do it the right way.

Andy remembered when he was very young and his mom and dad took a trip to Yellowstone Park. He even remembered the postcard they sent with a bear and her cub on it. It didn't matter that it arrived in the mail two days after his parents got home.

Andy was left in the care of Ned and Donna. Everything was fine until he awoke late Saturday night and his mother wasn't there. The longer he lay in bed the worse he felt. Finally, crying, he went to Ned's room. He told Ned he was scared and didn't want to sleep alone, and Ned let him sleep with him all night. Ned talked to him for a long time and then let Andy snuggle up against him all night. Andy felt safe and secure. He didn't even wake up when Ned got up in the morning to do the chores and milk the cows.

Ned was the handsome one in the family. He was also Mom's favorite. She took his side every time there was a problem. Dad, however, seemed to like Donna best. When Dad and Donna argued, Donna always got her way. Mom said they were just alike, both stubborn as mules. Andy didn't know where he fit in. Ned was the only one who stood up for him.

Although he was a year and a half younger than Donna, by his mid-teens Ned was taller than her. Andy thought Ned was very tall. He was even taller than Dad. He had nice regular features and his sandy hair was wavy. Andy remembered how great Ned looked in his uniform when he was home on furlough last fall. His hair was cut very short and he was very suntanned. He had also put on some weight, but it wasn't fat, it was muscle.

The Saturday before his furlough was over Ned took Andy fishing and they talked about all sorts of things.

"When I get back to the Army base, I will be shipping out. The Army is sending me overseas to the Philippine Islands to fight in the war," Ned said.

"Really? I sure hope you don't get hurt."

"Don't worry, Andy. I promise I'll come home, and when I do we'll go fishing again."

Andy waved to Ned as he carried his duffle bag up the street to catch the streetcar to the city. Ned waved back and then saluted. He was so big and handsome. Andy really looked forward to next summer when Ned would get out of the Army and come home. He couldn't wait to go fishing with Ned.

July came in hot. They said the weather for the annual 4th of July celebration at the town park would probably be well into the nineties. Andy and Ray were busily preparing for their yearly campout at Parker's Grove on the foothills east of town. Each year for the last two years the boys spent a couple of days after the 4th of July celebration on a camping trip. Ray's older brother had gone with them in the past, but this year, after much coaxing and pleading with their parents, they were to be allowed to go by themselves.

The pea crop had been harvested, and the corn and beets had been cultivated and hoed. It was between irrigation times for the fields, and July 4th fell after the first crop of hay had been harvested and before the second cutting, so this was a slow week on the farm. Dad could handle the chores for two days and agreed to let the boys go camping.

Andy dreaded it but he knew he had to talk with Linda, the girl who lived across the street from Uncle Jed's place. The first year they went camping she was the only person he could find who would drive his herd for him. He dreaded seeing her because she wanted far too much money to drive for the two days than he wanted to pay. Even though the cows knew their way to the pasture and home, someone had to open and lock the gates. Linda wanted fifty cents a day. He had to pay her a dollar for two days, and Andy would only make three dollars for the rest of the month. It wasn't fair. This year he didn't even try to get her to lower the price. He just agreed to her terms.

July 3rd, a Thursday, was spent gathering equipment, airing out sleeping bags, finding a hatchet, packing food and toilet paper and taking his pocketknife down to Mr. Harris at the garage to be sharpened. Usually Ned sharpened the knife for him, but he was gone and Dad was busy.

Mr. Harris was Andy's friend. Andy used to hang around the service station a lot, but his mother put a stop to that because she thought he was hearing far too much for his own good from the farmers who used the garage as a meeting place and hangout. Mr. Harris didn't seem to mind if Andy was there and neither did Mr. Otis who was often there, but Mother said no and that was that.

Andy told Mr. Harris about his camping plans while Mr. Harris was sharpening the knife. Mr. Harris warned him to be careful because there was not much rain during early spring and summer and the ground was very dry. The conditions were perfect for the rattlesnakes to move down from the hills to the bench land for water from the canal and better hunting. He said one farmer found three snakes while harvesting the first crop of hay on his dry farm. Andy thought it was a hell of a thing to be told a couple of days before his trip. He didn't like snakes. In fact, he was scared to death of them. He only heard a rattlesnake once, but the moment he heard it he knew what it was. Damn. He and Ray planned on climbing on the rocks on the south side of Cedar Hill, but if snakes had moved down he wasn't going near the place.

There was too much gear for them to carry so they decided to ride horses and let them carry the grub and equipment. Andy knew he could get Uncle Jed's horse, Old Red. Andy wasn't too crazy about horses in the first place, and he was even less thrilled about Old Red. Uncle Jed often told Andy he could ride the horse when he was driving cows for him, but Andy preferred his bicycle. Old Red was the only horse Andy knew he could borrow. The horse just wasn't ridden often enough to be gentle, and Andy was apprehensive about taking him and so was his mother; but Dad said it would be okay.

The problem was if that horse ever saw a snake or got a stick caught between his hind legs Andy would be thrown so far they would be hunting for him for a week. He heard the stories about the horse when he was listening to the men at the service station. In the valley Old Red was fine if he didn't get spooked. Most of the time he just stood around with no energy like he was about to give up the ghost, but get him in the mountains and he became a different animal. In mountain terrain he was high-spirited, sure-footed, a fine animal unless, unless he got spooked by a snake or a stick.

Uncle Jed suggested Andy ride the horse a couple of times before the trip. It would calm him down and let Andy get used to being on him so Andy decided he would ride Old Red to drive the cows. On the morning of the 4th of July he left his bicycle by Uncle Jed's corral and bridled the horse. He couldn't manage the saddle so he rode bareback. The horse was docile and everything was going smoothly. If he'd known how easy it was to control Old Red he would have ridden him to pasture all last summer. In fact, it was kind of fun riding the old horse, and the morning drive went well.

Andy left the baseball game about five o'clock and bicycled to his uncle's to get the horse. Old Red seemed a bit edgy as Andy headed him down the main road toward the pasture. The horse was too fat. Andy bounced each time the horse did. He knew the damn horse was bouncing on purpose. He was glad everyone was at the celebration and couldn't see how silly he looked bouncing down the street.

He crossed the highway and headed down the lower road. The sky was clouding over and the air was getting muggy. Andy hoped a storm was not coming just when they were going camping.

When he passed Charlie's pasture on the way down to open the gate for Dad's herd, he saw that Charlie's cows were in the back of the pasture. He opened the gate for Dad's cows and they started up the road toward home. At Charlie's pasture Andy slid off Old Red, unlocked the gate and walked it open. The cows were still in the back of the pasture. They occasionally stayed at the back if the front of the pasture was being irrigated or if there was an interruption in their day, like a thunderstorm, and they were still grazing. Andy climbed on the support for the gatepost to help him mount the old horse. It would be easier to get the cows today with Old Red. Without him Andy would have to get his feet wet walking out to get the cows in the boggy pasture, but today he could ride to the back of the pasture and not get wet.

Andy barely nudged the horse, turned him and they started toward the cows, when the horse broke into a dead run. Andy almost fell off when the horse bolted. He tugged on the reins to stop the horse but Old Red had his head down and Andy couldn't get leverage. The horse lurched forward and Andy grabbed his mane with his left hand to keep from falling. He lost his grip on the reins and grabbed the mane with both hands. Because the horse was not saddled and Andy's legs couldn't tighten onto the horse's fat body they flailed as he tried to find some kind of hold. Andy, his heart pounding and screaming for the horse to stop, held on for dear life. The horse sped to the back of the pasture, came to the fence and stopped in his tracks. Andy sailed between the horse's ears. He held onto the mane until the force of his body plunging forward forced him to let go, but not before the summersault motion started. He flew off the horse, over the fence and landed not with a thud but with a splat. He was flat on his back in slimy swampy mud. The damn horse turned around headed for the gate and toward home.

Andy lay there for sometime, stunned. He couldn't hear a thing. His face was dry but that was the only dry thing on him. His entire body and the back of his head to just in front of his ears had been slammed into the mud. His ears were filled with mud. He pulled his hands free and tried to sit up, but the sucking sour-smelling mud held him. Andy was crying, not because he was hurt but because he was mad. He finally fought his way to his feet and crawled through the fence back into the pasture. The horse was gone. Charlie's cows were going through the gate and heading up the road toward the highway while Andy stood crying and swearing with black mud and ooze covering his entire body except his face.

Andy trudged toward home through the fields so no one would see him. He stopped when he came to a clear stream or ditch to try to wash off some of the mud. He was so angry he couldn't stop crying and great sobs shook his body. His cheeks ached and his nose ran. He stopped at an iron water artesian well just west of the highway to make one last effort to clean off the slimy mud. The water was clear but it smelled terrible. He wanted to stop crying but he couldn't. As he got up to continue his embarrassing trek, he almost stumbled into Charlie. He looked at the old man and began sobbing even harder.

Without a word Charlie held out his hand and Andy took it. Charlie led him up the lane so no one would see how embarrassed Andy was. When they reached Charlie's corral gate Andy saw Old Red calmly standing by Uncle Jed's corral gate.

"That son-of-a-bitch," Andy sobbed, "I'm going to kill that son-of-a-bitch."

Charlie, smiling to himself, locked the corral gate and led Andy through the barnyard and up the path to the bench by the coal shed.

"Take off your shoes and shirt," Charlie said and disappeared around the corner of the house.

Andy, who had finally stopped sobbing, sat on the bench and did as he was told. Moments later Charlie returned with a garden hose and a towel. He threw the towel on top of the one that hung next to the faucet and attached the hose to the faucet. He told Andy to put the shoes and shirt on the lawn. He sprayed the mud off of them. Then he hosed down Andy.

Charlie gave him a towel and said, "Go in the shed and take of the rest off your clothes and give them to me."

There was even mud in his shorts. The back pockets of his jeans were full of moss and mud. Andy threw his pants and shorts on the lawn and the old man sprayed them with the hose.

Andy's ears were full of mud. Charlie took Andy into the house and into the bathroom he seldom used, and as gently as he could bent Andy's head over the basin and washed the mud from his ears.

He drew water in the tub and told Andy to get in. Charlie took the towel from around Andy's waist and Andy settled into the hot water. Charlie gave him some soap from a confectioner's jar on a shelf, took another towel from the cupboard, hung it next to the tub and left the bathroom.

The ball of soap was homemade. Charlie's wife made it. The odor was the one he smelled on the day of his fall. It was her bath soap. Andy looked around the bathroom and had a strange feeling he had been in the room before.

The kitchen door closed. The old man had gone outside.

It was Donna. Now Andy remembered when he was in this bathroom. He also remembered what Charlie's wife looked like. Donna used to dress Bessie's hair. He came over with Donna one day when she was tending him. He was very young then, maybe three; but he remembered the old lady put him in the bathtub while Donna was fixing her hair. There was no water in the bathtub. The old lady said she didn't want him running around the house. It made Donna very angry. That's why he remembered the day. Donna was so angry when they got home she screamed and cursed at the old lady. She and his mother had an argument over the incident.

Andy finished bathing, dried himself and cleaned the tub the best he could. He didn't want to leave a mess. He walked into the kitchen. The towel around his waist almost dragged on the floor it was so large. Charlie was not there but there was a pair of trousers and a small collarless pinstriped shirt lying on the chair next to the bathroom door. He rolled up the pant legs twice and the shirtsleeves to his elbows. The clothes were old fashioned. Andy had never seen any like them. They looked something like the ones worn by the children in the old family photographs on the chest in his mother's bedroom.

He went out to the bench by the coal shed, closing the kitchen door behind him. His clothes hung on the line by the shed and his shoes were stuck on the tops of two fence posts. Andy felt the clothes. The shirt was already almost dry, but the heavy jeans were still very wet.

Andy sat on the bench. He was glad Charlie hadn't sent him home. Everyone bathed this morning before going to the 4th of July celebration, and there had been no fire in the stove all day so there would be no hot water at his house, and his mother wasn't there to help him. She was still at the celebration, and his dad was out in the barnyard doing the evening chores. Andy was going to catch hell for not being there to help with the chores but he didn't care. He was glad Charlie let him take a bath. It was giving Andy a chance to get to know him a little. Maybe he would get to see the arrowhead collection after all.

He saw the old man a few times as he went about the routine of the evening milking. Things had happened so fast that Andy hadn't thought about anything except his embarrassment and getting the stinking mud off him. Charlie hadn't laughed at him. He just wanted to help and this time, unlike the time he fell, Andy let him. He was going to stick around until Charlie finished his chores.

When he was in the kitchen, Andy saw the old man's rocking chair in the corner, and there were newspapers taped to the floor around it. The story Mrs. West told back on Memorial Day was true. Andy wished it wasn't.

As the cows began filing out of the barn into the corral Andy got up from the bench and started down the path toward the barnyard. He didn't want to bother the old man while he was milking. Charlie certainly milked in a hurry. Either that or he was not milking all of the cows. It could be some of them were in their dry period, the few months rest given all cows before they calved.

Andy opened the barn door and the long rays of the setting sun lit up the inside of the barn. Charlie finished pouring a sack of rolled barley into the bin and shook the bag to loosen the last of the grain. Dust billowed into the amber light. Andy stood silhouetted in the doorway.

The old man was startled for a moment and there was a strange look on his face when he emerged through the dust cloud. Then he said, "Feeling better now?"

"Yes, thank you. And thanks for helping me," Andy replied. His eyes began to fill with tears again.

"You're welcome," Charlie said and walked past Andy into the barnyard.

Andy followed and Charlie latched the barn door behind them. He picked up the handle of the iron-wheeled milk cart with two cans from the evening milking in it. There were nine cows and only two cans of milk so some of the cows must be dry or close to it.

As Charlie started toward the cooling trough Andy fell in behind and assisted him by pushing the cart. The old man looked over his shoulder and Andy hesitated before continuing to push. Andy watched Charlie lift one and then the other can of milk and put them in the water. Either he was very strong or the cans were not full. No wonder he finished milking so fast.

"Are these your clothes?" Andy asked.

"No they belonged to my brother. He died years ago when he was about your age," the old man said.

"He must have been bigger than me," Andy said, "How did he die?"

"He fell off a horse."

A group of cars came down the street. The celebration at the park was over, and the families were coming home for dinner before going to the fireworks show. An automobile filled with some of his friends went past. Andy recognized Dad's car coming across the streetcar tracks. Donna was probably driving.

Andy went to the clothesline and took down his clothes. The jeans were still wet so he asked if he could change at home and bring back the clothes he was wearing later. Charlie said yes and crossed to the fence and got Andy's shoes off the posts.

"My family is going to the fireworks tonight. Would you like to come with us?" Andy asked.

The old man handed him the shoes and shook his head.

"But I know they would like you to come," Andy said.

"Thank you, boy," Charlie said, "but I couldn't."

Andy took the shoes, thanked him again and went home.

Dad was mad because Andy wasn't there to do his chores. He calmed down when Andy told Dad what happened to him and Old Red at the pasture. Dad laughed but his mother didn't. She said she was worried that something terrible would happen when Andy went camping.

He threw his jeans in the dirty clothes hamper and got a clean pair from the drawer. His shirt was dry but it was stiff from the mud that wasn't washed out by the hose and it smelled terrible. He got his striped pullover out of his drawer and his Sunday shoes and changed clothes.

His mother looked at the pinstriped collarless shirt and the twill wool pants. They were from the 1880's. She asked Andy about them and he told her that Charlie said they belonged to his brother.

"Why these are Ben's clothes," she said.

VIII

Charlie felt a surge of relief when he saw the boy sitting by the iron water well. He had seen the boy get the old red horse from Jed's corral. He never liked the animal. He didn't trust him. Later when the horse came up the lane with the reins dragging, he was concerned. When his herd arrived at the corral and the boy was not with them he feared something was terribly wrong. If something happened on the stretch of main road between the highway and the turnoff to his place, someone would have found the boy. It must have happened down at the pasture because the horse came home so much sooner than the cows.

Charlie took the shortcut through the fields to get to the pasture as fast as possible. He was hurrying through a field, his heart pounding when he heard sobbing. He walked to the edge of the willows to see if it was the boy and to find out what had happened. The sight of the boy covered with mud and slime trying desperately to clean it off, sobbing uncontrollably and cursing up a storm was very funny. He wanted to laugh, but he knew the humiliation and embarrassment the boy felt and he couldn't.

Later in the barn when Charlie saw the boy through the grain dust and silhouetted in the barn doorway, something stirred in his memory. For a moment the figure looked familiar to him, and then he realized what it was about the boy. He looked like Ben.

The boy needed clothes so Charlie went to the trunk. A flood of memories poured out when he opened it. He hadn't opened it for years, how many he didn't remember; but when he did all the memories leapt out, the memories of his life with his brother Ben.

The trunk, assorted pieces of furniture and a few storage boxes from the attic were brought home by Charlie after his mother died. His sister took all the valuable items, but that was all right with Charlie. He wanted nothing that belonged to his parents. He picked up the things left behind by his sister at the request of the people who bought the house.

Bessie was upset when he claimed nothing from the estate. She looked anxiously through the trunk and boxes when Charlie brought them home but found nothing of particular value. It was Bessie who told him Ben's clothing was in the trunk. Charlie didn't want to throw away Ben's things so forty years ago he put the trunk in the spare bedroom, and it had been there ever since.

He knelt by the trunk and opened it. The clothing, two pair of trousers, three shirts and a vest, were on top of the other things. The clothes were pressed and neatly folded. They smelled musty. He remembered seeing Ben wearing the clothes. Charlie took the clothes and put them on the bed.

Other items in the trunk stirred more memories. Wrapped in a cloth and carefully tucked between a shoebox and some kind of coat was a bronze-plated pot metal horse that was Ben's prized possession. Ben won the horse at the county fair by throwing pennies onto flat dishes and getting one to stay on the dish in the center of the game board. The horse was tarnished and there was rust where the brass plating was chipped, and the crack still showed where the tail had been broken off.

Memories of his childhood came flooding back. The image of Ben's smiling face and the sound of his laughter filled Charlie's head. He had pushed the memory of his brother out of his mind years ago. Ben died in the summer of 1878 when he was twelve years old and Charlie was ten. Ben was an extraordinary person, and although he had been dead for more than sixty years the memory of his smile and infectious laugh made Charlie smile.

He had forgotten about the horse and how Ben told him he could play with it. Ben said to be very careful but Charlie dropped it. He was young and the horse was heavier than he anticipated. He lifted it from the bookcase shelf and it slipped from his grasp. It struck tail first on the bare wood floor and broke.

Ben did not yell at him. Ben never yelled or got angry with anyone. He simply picked up the horse and went outdoors. Charlie followed saying how sorry he was, but Ben ran down the path and into the barn. Charlie was not able to keep up and Ben locked the barn door. Charlie didn't see him for the entire afternoon. Around dinnertime Ben walked up the path, smiled at Charlie and went into the living room and placed the broken horse back on the bookcase shelf.

That night in bed Charlie was still feeling guilty about what happened. He laid on the edge of the bed with his back toward Ben. Ben, without a word, reached over and put his arm around Charlie. Charlie knew everything was all right. The following day Ben glued the tail back on the horse as best he could and the incident was never mentioned again.

Ben was like no person Charlie ever knew. Their mother said Ben was just too good for this world. This was, of course, after he was dead; but to Charlie he was everything good and kind. Ben was everyone's favorite, especially his father's; and Charlie knew his father blamed him for Ben's death.

Ben was driving cows for Charlie the day it happened. Charlie wanted to stay at a birthday party, and Ben offered to bring both his herd and Charlie's from the pasture. He was on the old roan mare riding the fence line to get the cows from the back of the pasture. Ben was an excellent horseman. He always rode bareback. The roan was a big horse and Ben's legs didn't reach very far around the sides of the horse, but he sat the horse like he was glued on to it.

Whether it was heel flies or the horse stepped into a hole in the boggy pasture nobody knew, but something caused the horse to buck or make a sudden move sideways. Ben fell off onto the barbed wire fence and the barbs tore open his throat. He was found between the back of the pasture and the gate, yards away from the bloody barbs. The doctor said he either bled to death or drowned in his own blood.

Charlie and Ben were closer than most brothers; they were best friends. The family never talked much, but Ben and Charlie talked about everything. They shared the big iron bed in the upstairs bedroom and spent many nights talking about their dreams for the future. Charlie loved Ben more than anyone in the world. First there was Ben and then there was Bessie. They were Charlie's whole life, and now they were both gone.

Charlie had driven Ben's herd for a week so Ben could go to the city to visit their cousins, and to return the favor Ben offered to get Charlie's herd that evening so he could stay at the party.

After the party Charlie went home to find many wagons in front of his house. From a distance he saw people gathered around one of the buckboards. His mother was helped off the back of the wagon; she was sobbing uncontrollably. His father enfolded her in his arms and stood staring stoically at something or someone wrapped in a blanket in the buckboard.

Charlie's heart stopped. He knew it was Ben. He pushed through the crowd and, before anyone could stop him, he leapt onto the back of the wagon and pulled back the blanket. Ben's blood-smeared face was bloodless and gray. Charlie gazed in disbelief. Someone pried the blanket from his grasp and covered the lifeless body. Charlie's gaze went to the silent, motionless crowd and he searched each face. As his eyes met theirs they turned away or lowered their heads. Then his eyes met his father's eyes. He did not turn away. There was hatred and accusation in his eyes as he stared straight at Charlie. Charlie burst into tears and cried that he was sorry, but his father continued to gaze at him.

The next few days were a blur. Charlie remembered little of what he said or did. Even years later the events were still unclear. After the funeral the feelings of guilt began gnawing at him, and it was made even worse by the loneliness he felt. Charlie couldn't understand why he felt or should feel guilty. He didn't understand why his father would blame him; hate him. He told his mother what happened and how he felt, and she said he must be mistaken. She was certain his father didn't blame him or hate him. Although nothing was ever said, Charlie remembered the accusing look that never left his father's eyes.

He never saw his father cry, not even at Ben's funeral. Didn't he love Ben either? His mother said of course he loved Ben but men just didn't cry, and he would understand when he grew up.

Charlie lived with the guilt for years. He grew away from his parents and became sullen and moody. He fluctuated between loving and hating Ben. It was only after much time and with Bessie's help that he was able to accept that he was not to blame for the accident, but in the process he pushed his family away and the memory of Ben out of his consciousness. Now remembering after so much time had passed, hurt welled up inside of him. How different his life would have been if Ben had been there to share it.

The evening sun heated the west side of the house and the heat was beginning to radiate into the spare bedroom. Charlie closed the trunk and went to the kitchen. It was stifling. He opened the kitchen door but there was no breeze. He splashed water from the faucet by the coal shed on his face and wiped it off with the green towel. He hung the towel on the peg and sat down. The bench had been in the shade for most of the afternoon and was cool. The images of childhood and Ben again filled his mind and he was soon lost in memories.

IX

Andy stood on the rickety fence while Ray tried to keep it from moving. The back screen door of old man Grant's house flew open and banged against the siding, and Grant bellowed, "Get the hell out of those apples or I'll kick your ass."

Ray ran leaving Andy with all of his back pockets and the inside of his shirt filled with apples. He had an apple in one hand and with the other hand he clung to a shaky tree branch. He tried to keep his balance and climb off the swaying fence. Mr. Grant hadn't seen him clearly enough to know who he was, and if Andy could get down and make it to Uncle Jed's barn, he would be safe. The branch bent under his weight and Andy leaned forward to keep his balance. If he had to fall he wanted to fall outside of Grant's yard and not into it. He tugged at the limb, dropped the apple in his hand and was using his free arm to help regain his balance when the fence collapsed.

He hit the ground with a thud and Grant, the grouchiest man in town, was upon him. Andy wasn't hurt, but now the old man really had something to yell about. He wouldn't do much about swiping a few apples, but he sure in hell could and would do something about the broken fence.

Mr. Grant grabbed Andy and pulled him to his feet. The seat of Andy's pants caught on a nail, and when the old man lifted him the whole seat of Andy's pants ripped. The old man kicked his behind hard and apples tumbled from his pockets and the inside of his shirt. In the fall the weight of the apples popped off the buttons on the front of Andy's shirt. Mr. Grant held him by the arm screaming about paying for the damage. He would see Andy's father, the boy would be punished and the fence would have to be repaired.

Andy tried to tell the old man he was sorry and that the fence would be fixed. He pleaded with him not to tell his father, but Grant wouldn't listen. He knew he had won. The harangue stopped as abruptly as it began. Mr. Grant picked up the apples and stormed into the house.

Damn, there goes my camping trip, Andy thought to himself. Dad would sure as hell not let him go after this incident. Andy had made old man Grant's summer. He was going to get his fence fixed and probably thought he was getting even with one of the kids who teased him, but Andy wasn't one of those who teased the old man. In fact, he didn't go with the boys to tease anyone. He hadn't done so since the day he was with the kids when they were talking about old Charlie when Charlie could hear them.

All Andy wanted was a few apples, and it wasn't even his idea to swipe them. It was Ray's idea. Damn Ray. And Ray didn't even have to help fix the fence. He wouldn't help even if Andy asked him for fear old man Grant would recognize him as one of the kids who loved to tease him.

The kick didn't hurt. Either Andy hadn't been kicked very hard or he was so scared that it didn't even register that he'd been kicked. Andy looked down at the front of his shirt with no buttons and saw the flap hanging down from the back of his pants. He looked like hell. He shoved his hands into his pockets and took a shortcut through the backyards to get home so no one would see him with his butt hanging out.

He knew Mr. Grant would sure as hell have been on the telephone with his father by the time he got home. He was kind of surprised the old man didn't take him home and make a big stink. What was he going to tell Dad? There was probably going to be a lot of yelling and screaming about stealing and how he was going to wind up in jail someday. Andy knew he would have to pay for the fence repairs out of his cow-driving money. It was all so embarrassing. The only things he was really sorry about were that he wouldn't be going camping and he wouldn't have any money to spend.

Andy crossed Uncle Jed's calf pasture and climbed the fence to the corral. Old Whitey was lying next to the watering trough. She didn't move when Andy passed. Either she recognized him or she was just too lazy to get up. Andy went back and put his hand on the cow's side. She looked at him and reached out her nose toward him but still made no effort to get up. She remembered him. He slapped her on the side. *Maybe cows aren't so dumb after all.*

Andy climbed over the gate. He was trying to figure out how he was going to explain to his dad what happened with old man Grant. He hoped he didn't get Ray into trouble too, but most of all he hoped he would still be allowed to go on the camping trip. He climbed over the fence to Charlie's corral and spoke to the cows as he crossed the corral. He squeezed through one of the stalls in the manger. The cows had tossed the hay out of reach so with the broken handled pitchfork he pulled from the haystack he pushed the hay back in the manger. Some of the cows got up to come and eat. He threw the pitchfork back into the haystack, pretending the stack was old man Grant. He crossed the barnyard and started up the path toward Charlie's house and was cursing Grant under his breath when he became aware he was being watched. He heard a low chuckle and saw Charlie sitting on the bench by the coal shed with a towel. Charlie was laughing.

Embarrassed that his pants didn't have a seat in them, Andy pulled the hanging flap over the gap and continued up the path with both hands in his back pockets holding the flap in place. He tried to act natural and smiled when he approached Charlie.

The boy was such a pathetic little sight coming through the corral with the flap that used to be the seat of his pants hanging down and bouncing off the back of his leg with each step he took. His shirt was hanging open and he looked like he had been in a fight and lost. It seemed every time Charlie saw the boy he had just had some sort of accident. Charlie couldn't help laughing.

"I saw you climb over the fence to the corral," Charlie said, "I heard Grant yelling at someone and figured there were some kids in his apple trees again, but I didn't figure it would be you. Did Grant catch you or did you have an accident?"

Andy walked to the bench and sat beside Charlie. He jumped when the cool bench touched his skin through the hole in his pants. Andy giggled and Charlie laughed.

"Yep," Andy said, "I kind of tore the seat out of my pants. Well, actually I didn't. Old man Grant did."

It surprised Charlie that Andy would tell him about swiping apples, how the fence broke and how he fell. The boy was so open about what he did. Charlie liked that very much. He felt good when he was around the boy. Although he didn't look very much like Ben, there was something about his clear blue eyes and the way he looked directly at you without the slightest hint of guilt or self-consciousness that put Charlie at ease. It was a quality his brother possessed.

It had been so long since Charlie talked with anyone. He felt awkward and didn't know how to keep a conversation going. He enjoyed the boy telling his story, but when the story was over there was an uneasy silence. Charlie wanted to say something but was at a loss. He felt like escaping into the house, but he wanted the conversation to continue.

Andy broke the silence. "Can I see your arrowhead collection sometime? Mr. Otis told me about your collection when he helped me when I lost your cow the first day I drove them to the pasture." As soon as he said it Andy remembered Charlie didn't know about that, but Charlie smiled and Andy knew it was all right.

The tension was gone, and now that Charlie had something to talk about, he was eager to pick up the conversation.

"Would you like to see it now?" Charlie asked.

The boy's eyes lit up. "Sure," Andy said. He was in no hurry to go home and face Dad.

Charlie smiled. Bill Otis was right. The boy really was interested and wanted to be with him.

They went into the living room. It was the room where Andy woke up on the day he fell and hit his head. He still felt bad about the way he acted. He looked at Charlie, but with the low light in the room he couldn't tell if Charlie was looking back at him. In a sudden outburst Andy said, "I really apologize for the way I acted when you helped me the day I fell." Just like the day he asked for the job driving cows, he found himself talking too loud and too fast.

Charlie smiled at the boy. "It's all right," he said, "there is no need to apologize.

He took a wooden box from the sideboard and motioned for Andy to follow him. They went into the kitchen where there was better light and Andy knelt on a chair next to Charlie and rested his elbows on the table. Charlie removed some arrowheads and lined them up on the table. There were more arrowheads in the box than Andy had ever seen before.

"Wow these are great," Andy said, "Where did you get them?"

There were many black obsidian arrowheads that were fairly common in the area, but there were also rust and green-colored flint arrowheads; and some gray-colored ones as well.

"When I was a boy there were arrowheads all over the place," Charlie said. "Before the white man got to the valley, this place was a hunting ground for lots of Indian tribes. They'd hunted in this valley for hundreds of years because there were animals everywhere. Because there are so many springs there was lots of food and water for them. The Indians would come to the valley to stock up on meat for their winter supply of jerky. They didn't always hit what they were shooting at, and sometimes the arrows got lost in the brush or the grass. Sometimes when they killed an animal the arrowhead broke off in the animal and got discarded with the guts. After the scavengers picked over the innards the arrowhead was left on the ground."

"How did you know where to look?" Andy asked.

"The best place to find arrowheads was around watering holes. I found most of those black ones by that spring about a block up from my pasture. It was in my dad's pasture and I played at the spring a lot.'

"What about this one?" Andy asked, picking up a beautiful rust-colored arrowhead that was larger than most of the others.

"I found that one down on the Bear River," Charlie said. "I don't know for sure, but I think it must be from a fishing spear. After the runoff one spring, I saw it laying on the clay bottom of a stream where it emptied into the river."

"It's a beauty."

"I didn't find all of them. When I was a boy, all the kids collected arrowheads and we would trade them so that we all got all the different kinds. I traded a kid for those green ones. He found them while he was working one summer on his grandfather's farm up north. We never knew which of the tribes made those.

"Do you think there were battles between the tribes?" Andy asked.

"There could have been. I'm not sure but I know some of the tribes didn't get along at all," Charlie said.

"Were there arrowheads in town?"

"Sure. They were everywhere. We didn't just find them by the watering holes. When we were in the fields hoeing corn or thinning sugar beets, we found a lot too. Every time a field got plowed some relics would turn up," Charlie said.

He laughed and held up an arrowhead that had a piece of buckskin strap around the base. "I found this arrowhead when I was topping sugar beets one fall. The roots of a large beet had grown around it like a fist. I could only see the base and the piece of buckskin sticking out. The strip of buckskin is what's left of the strap that secured the arrowhead to the shaft."

"Wow!"

Charlie picked up another grayish arrowhead and said, "I found this one imbedded in a log. I was splitting firewood for the winter and it popped out of the log."

They talked until well after dark.

"Andy," a voice called from across the street.

Andy recognized the yell of his obviously irritated dad. He didn't want to go home. He'd been having such a good time he forgot about the apple incident, but he also forgot to help Dad with the chores. He knew he had better get home fast and face his father before he made it worse.

"I'd better get home and face the music," Andy said, "I'm sure old man Grant has talked to my dad, and I'm going to catch all kinds of hell."

Charlie laughed.

Andy had barely inspected half the contents of the box.

"Thanks for showing me the collection. Can I come back sometime and see the rest of them?"

Charlie nodded his approval. "Come over anytime you want, Andy."

Andy said goodbye and disappeared through the front gate. Charlie stood in the kitchen doorway and watched the boy as he ran across the street. He was pleased. He couldn't remember the last time he had talked so much. He enjoyed it. He enjoyed Andy, and he was pleased that they were becoming friends.

X

Andy went directly home from taking the cows to pasture and sat down to eat breakfast. The thought of facing Mr. Grant made him a little sick to his stomach. He wanted so badly to get the ordeal over and done with that he couldn't finish his meal.

Last night was as bad as Andy expected. He was certain half the town heard his father yelling at him. If Dad was right he was going to hell for sure.

Dad was not only angry about old man Grant's fence, he was mad about Andy stealing apples and really mad that Andy would not be going to work with him in the field. There was a lot that had to be done before the harvest of second crop hay.

Andy was told in no uncertain terms that the camping trip was off. Dad insisted that he call Ray and explain why they were not going camping so Andy spent quite awhile on the telephone with Ray. After a lot of coaxing and a few threats Ray agreed to meet him at nine o'clock to help with the fence repairs. Andy not only had to pay for repairing the fence out of his cow-driving money, but Dad, who didn't know Ray was involved, made him promise to pay Ray for the time he worked. With the amount of work old man Grant was bound to give him, he would be working for the next two years to pay for everything.

Andy leaned his bicycle against the picket fence. The fence paint was peeling, and he knew while Grant had him in his clutches he would probably be painting the front yard fence as well. The gate sagged and the porch railing was void of paint and weathered. The whole place looked like one big repair job to Andy. He knew he was going to have to spend the entire summer working for the old man, and all for a few damned apples he never got to keep.

He knocked on the front door and thought about running away for a few years until everything was forgotten, but it was too late. He heard footsteps coming toward the door and resigned himself to a summer of hard labor.

Andy could tell old man Grant was getting tremendous enjoyment out of his suffering. As they walked through the backyard to the apple trees, he told Andy he wanted all the posts reset and the railings and pickets replaced. Andy thought the old man was being unfair. The fence had not been repaired for a hundred years, and now the old fart wanted it as good as new.

Mr. Grant finished giving him instructions on what was to be done. The list was endless. Andy would be working through October to finish. The old man left Andy with the admonition that, although he was going to be working in the field, he expected to see real progress on the fence by the time he returned for evening chores or else. Andy wanted to say, "or else what?" but he knew it would only provoke the old man so he held his tongue.

Andy began doing what he was told to do. *Where in hell is Ray?* He couldn't lift the rails without some help. Andy began pulling nails from the rails and pickets and stacking the pickets near the part of the fence that was still standing.

Soon after Andy started working Mr. Grant came out of the back door, scanned the situation, went to the barnyard where he hitched up his team of horses and left for the south field.

Andy worked for what seemed like an hour, but Ray didn't show up to help. The nails were out of all the pickets and most of the rails. Ray was nowhere in sight. Andy decided to ride over to Ray's house to see what was keeping him, and then he saw Charlie coming across the pasture. He had a shovel over his shoulder and a hammer in the loop of the carpenter's apron tied around his waist.

"Need some help?" Charlie asked.

Andy began explaining about Ray but Charlie said not to worry about him. They could fix the fence together.

Andy did most of the talking and Charlie did most of the work. Charlie looked at the boy in amazement. The kid never seemed to run out of things to say. By noon the posts were reset and the rails nailed to them.

Andy had lunch at Charlie's house. Charlie was a little embarrassed by what he served, but it was all he had. It was an unusual lunch for Andy but he liked it. Charlie gave him a plate with store-bought bread, butter and jam, some fresh green onions and radishes from the garden, a slice of cold ham and a glass of lemonade. Charlie saw how Andy seemed to relish his offering and it pleased him. He had never served food to anyone except Bessie. It seemed strange to be concerned with the opinion and approval of an eleven-year-old boy, but Charlie was.

By mid-afternoon the fence was repaired.

"Thanks for all the help," Andy said, "I couldn't have done it by myself."

"You're welcome."

"I can do the rest of the jobs by myself."

"Rest of the jobs? What jobs," Charlie asked.

Andy listed the things Mr. Grant told him he had to do.

"It's just like that old bastard to take advantage of a situation like this," Charlie said angrily. "You don't have to do any more. You've repaired his damn fence." He took a small pad from the bib pocket of his overalls. From the wire loops that held the pad together he extracted a stubby pencil. He handed them to Andy and asked him if he could write. Andy said he sure could, and Charlie told him to write a note saying: "He has done enough. If there were any complaints, talk to me."

Charlie put the note in the handle of the back screen door. They each picked two apples and headed for Charlie's place. As they crossed Uncle Jed's calf pasture toward Charlie's corral Andy asked why he didn't sign the note. Charlie lowered his head and told Andy he didn't sign because he couldn't write. He never learned to read or write because his father took him out of school to work on the farm. He said it was not unusual when Charlie was a boy for a family to do that.

Andy noticed Charlie always had a pad and pencil in his overalls bib pocket and a small book in his back pocket. The magazine rack next to his chair in the kitchen was filled with all kinds of magazines, but the most curious thing was that Charlie had the newspaper delivered every day. It was weird.

Charlie told Andy he was sure Andy wouldn't be bothered by old man Grant. It was Grant who refused to give the right of way for the lane to go all the way through the block. That was the reason Charlie's milk cans had to be taken to the stand by the street. The two men came to blows over the incident, and Charlie gave Grant two black eyes during the fight. He told Andy he would love to have one more shot at the old man. Grant knew it and never went any place where he might run into Charlie without other people around.

Andy laughed. He thought the image of the two old men standing toe to toe and battling it out was very funny.

After supper Andy retrieved his bike from in front of Mr. Grant's house and then went to Charlie's. They sat on the bench behind his house, and Andy listened to Charlie tell stories about growing up and what the town was like right after it was settled. His parents were among the first settlers, and Charlie was born when the town had only been settled for about ten years. He told Andy things about himself that he had never told anyone, except Bessie.

As Charlie finished a story about why he was taken out of school, Andy remembered what his mother told him to do so he said, "Mom said I have to ask you what you want me to call you? She said she didn't want me to be rude so I should ask."

"You can call me Charlie and I'll call you Andy. Okay?"

"Yeah."

Charlie told Andy about Ben and how much he missed him. He got the bronze-plated horse from the trunk and told the story about Ben winning the horse and how Charlie dropped it. He thought about giving it to the boy, but it meant so much to him he couldn't part with it. It brought up too many good memories.

Andy had never seen such a beautiful horse. He thought it was much prettier than the horses they had for prizes at the county fair nowadays.

The summer moon was high and the canyon breeze rustled the poplar leaves when Andy, still in a daze, said goodnight and went across the street to his home and bed.

The next day Charlie searched through the trunk. He wasn't certain, but he thought that somewhere in the bottom of the truck were the games he and Ben used to play. He could not find them and was about to give up when he remembered seeing them on the shelf at the back of the closet. He couldn't imagine why Bessie saved them but she had. He found a checkerboard and a box of checkers. There was a Chinese checker set including all the marbles, and there was a deck of cards.

During their next few evenings together they played games. Andy had played checkers and knew all the card games Charlie knew, but he had never played Chinese checkers and was anxious to learn. He liked the game a lot, and they had a great time.

While they played games Charlie continued to tell stories. Andy wanted to hear them all.

"What was the town like when you were young?" Andy asked.

"When I was a boy there were only about two hundred people in town," Charlie said, "There were not many big trees except for the willow trees that had always been here. Some of the fruit and shade trees the settlers planted were getting pretty big, but there were no poplar trees yet. There were no sidewalks and the main road to the highway was just a dirt road. There were no cars, and there really wasn't much to do in town. That was before they built the streetcar line. The steam train came through the valley, but the streetcar line wasn't built until about 1913."

"How did you get to the city before there was a streetcar?" Andy asked.

"We didn't go to the city very often because we had to go by wagon, and the trip took most of the day. We were too busy trying to grow enough food to stay alive to go to the city."

"What did you do if you needed something you could only get in the city?"

"There was a freight wagon business in the valley and once a week a wagon would come to town," Charlie said, "If you needed something you went over to the park where the wagon stopped and placed an order with the driver, and the next week they would bring it to you. If you had an emergency, like an equipment breakdown, you'd have to borrow the equipment from a neighbor or wait until the freight company brought a replacement. We were all in the same boat so we helped each other as much as we could. Things changed a lot after the streetcar line was built."

He told of planting the poplar trees and about the bad winters and the years of drought. He told stories of the town's scandals, its rebels and heroes.

One of the stories Charlie told Andy was about the animals that lived in the valley when he was a boy. When the pioneers came the place was called Willow Valley because all of the streams that flowed into it were lined with willow trees. The fur trappers who came to the valley to trap beaver in the 1830s named it. There were no beaver in the valley anymore, but there were some still up in the mountains. When he was fishing, Andy had seen the dams they built on the creeks that flowed into the river.

Charlie said the place was filled with all kinds of birds and animals. Game birds were everywhere. Geese, ducks, quail, grouse, mourning doves and many other birds were plentiful. The streams were teeming with fish. The native species in the streams were the brook trout, the cutthroat trout and the white fish. The river bottoms were full of carp, catfish and bass. Mountain sheep, deer and elk were everywhere; there were even a few buffalo. Grizzly bears, foxes and coyotes were plentiful.

Because of the abundance of game, the valley was prime hunting ground for the Indian tribes.

The cattle the pioneers brought were for breeding stock and to provide milk, and the steers were seldom slaughtered. They were raised and became the oxen that pulled wagons and plows. The farm animals were all too precious to be slaughtered for food so the pioneers lived on the game.

By the 1880s the game animals were disappearing. Because too many domestic sheep were allowed to graze on the mountains on the west side of the valley, the range was overgrazed and could not recover so the native mountain sheep left the area and moved north out of the valley.

The settlers fished out several streams in the north end of the valley. The brook trout were gone. It wasn't until the 1920s that they brought in fingerlings and closed fishing for several years. By that time the people were able to grow plenty of food and didn't rely on the game and fish to survive. Fishing became more of a sport than a necessity. A government agency was established to make certain the streams in the valley were never fished out again. It was named The Department of Fish and Game and it required people to purchase a fishing license, and it limited the number of trout that could be taken.

Because it wasn't easy in the 1880s to get up the canyons to fish the river and streams, the cutthroat trout were not fished out and way up near the head of the river the brook trout survived.

The grizzly bears in the valley were slaughtered because they were such a threat to the pioneers' safety. Those that were not killed were driven out of the valley and up into the mountains. The last known grizzly bear in the area was killed about the time Andy was born. It was high up in the mountains, but it was killing sheep so they hunted it down and killed it.

The coyotes and foxes moved to unsettled areas or to the mountains, but there were still plenty around.

There was also a tremendous overkill of the deer and elk. The elk disappeared first and in the 1890s the deer were gone. About the time the streams were restocked, elk were brought in from Wyoming and they started to rebuild the herd. It has grown, but there are very few permits issued to hunt elk because a bad winter could put the herd in danger.

The deer disappeared around the same time. A tremendous number of deer were slaughtered, and the remaining deer left the area. It wasn't until around 1920 that deer started to migrate back into the mountains, and hunting was prohibited for years to allow the herd to rebuild.

A lot of the men in town hunt deer, but the number of licenses is limited and only the buck can be taken. The older townspeople remember when there were no deer so they are very concerned about the health of the herd.

Charlie told Andy anything and everything that came to mind. He had never talked so much in his life. The more he talked, the more he remembered. He told of things he hadn't thought about for years. Andy sat motionless, caught up in the magic long after the red glow left the eastern mountains and the western sky.

Their friendship grew and whenever possible they spent evenings together. When Dad would let him, which wasn't very often because there was so much to do around their farm, Andy went to the fields with Charlie to help him hoe corn or irrigate the alfalfa.

There were nights when Charlie was too tired from working all day in the field to have company, and there were nights when Andy fell asleep waiting for Charlie to finish his chores.

Their best times were on the weekend. They often spent Saturday nights together and most of Sunday. Andy would have eaten every Sunday dinner with Charlie, but his mother wouldn't let him.

On Thursday Dad said he had to help one of his friends build a new corral fence so Andy was free to play all day. He and Ray went to the canal and played until it got too hot to be in the sun so they decided to go home where they could play in the shade.

They jumped on their bikes and as they rode past the Peterson place they saw a lot of cars parked in front of the house. Several men and women were standing in the yard talking. The front door was open and there were people in the living room. Andy wondered what was going on. It wasn't a bridge club because there were men there, and none of the Peterson kids were getting married so he couldn't figure out why all the people were there.

When they got to Andy's house they went inside to get a drink of water and to find out if Andy's mother knew what was going on at the Petersons'. She told them to sit down at the kitchen table, and she poured them each a glass of lemonade and sat down beside them.

"A terrible thing has happened," she said. "Greg Peterson was killed in action a few days ago. They got word this morning."

Andy knew ten men from the town, including Ned, were in the service. He also knew Greg was in the Marines, but he didn't know he had been sent overseas.

"Where did it happen?" Andy asked.

"Somewhere in the Philippines Islands."

Andy was sorry about Greg. He was a friend of Ned's, and he had been in Andy's house many times. Andy liked Greg a lot. He was really a nice guy.

The entire town mourned the death. It was all anyone talked about. Andy began to worry about Ned because he was in the Philippines, and he could be killed too. Andy couldn't stop thinking about his brother. Dad tried to assure Andy that Ned would be all right, but it didn't help.

Saturday evening after chores, Andy went to Charlie's. They talked about Greg's death, and they talked about the terrible things that happen in a war. Charlie told Andy stories about what happened during World War I.

Charlie was too old to be drafted, and he didn't enlist because he was married and had no children to run the farm; and Bessie couldn't run the place by herself.

Five men from town died in the war. Three were soldiers who died from poison gas attacks in France. The other two were shot in combat.

Andy told Charlie that he was worried about Ned. Charlie struggled to find something to say to help Andy cope with his fears; but he realized that nothing he said was helping.

Andy said that he was okay, but he knew he wasn't. He continued to worry, but he didn't tell anyone, not even his mother, that he often woke up in the middle of the night from a nightmare about Ned's death. He didn't go to his parents for comfort. He had to deal with it like a man.

One evening they sat at the kitchen table looking at Charlie's arrowhead collection. Andy inspected each of the arrowheads on display before him. He asked questions about them and sat spellbound as Charlie told him the history of each piece. One particular arrowhead fascinated him. It was a very small one and, although it was made of black obsidian, it was so thin it was almost transparent at the edges and translucent in the middle. Andy couldn't imagine how anyone using rustic tools could fashion such a delicate object.

Charlie told Andy the Indians didn't really use many tools in making the arrowheads. Most of the finish work was done with water. They heated an arrowhead in the campfire and when the obsidian was hot they dropped a single drop of cold water onto the spot where they wanted to remove a chip. When the cold water hit the hot obsidian it would cause a fracture where the droplet touched. In this way the arrowhead was slowly shaped.

"Would you like to have that one?" Charlie asked.

"You mean I can have it?"

Charlie nodded.

"Oh boy," Andy said, "Thanks, thanks a lot."

They finished exploring the rest of the collection, and it was past Andy's bedtime when he thanked Charlie again for the great gift and went home.

The next day Andy found a piece of soft cloth in his mother's quilt scrap box and carefully wrapped the arrowhead in it. It would be his good luck piece. He would carry it always. It fit nicely in the money pocket of his jeans.

Charlie was pleased Andy was so delighted with the gift. He decided he would surprise Andy by making another gift. Because Andy was so drawn to Ben's bronze horse, he decided to use it as a model and carve one out of wood for the boy.

When he was a young man Charlie whittled and carved a lot of things, and he developed quite a skill as a woodcarver. He had not attempted to carve anything since long before Bessie died, but he wanted to try making a horse.

He rummaged through the cabinet in the shed and found the canvas bag wrapped up and securely tied with twine. With his pocketknife he cut the cording and removed the carving chisels and knives. The implements had a few rust spots on them and they were dull, but with a little work they would do nicely.

The farm demanded most of his time so the project went slowly. He found little time to carve during the day, and when he had time in the evening Andy was usually there. Lunchtime was the best and almost only opportunity he had to work on the horse. It began to take shape. The roughing in process went quickly, but he found it took time and a great deal of effort for his old hands to manipulate the knife to carve the detail work. He was enjoying the project and slowly his carving technique improved.

On hot evenings in late July Charlie and Andy often sat on the bench outside the coal shed or on the porch steps and talked. Charlie had never talked so much. Even with Ben he had not talked so freely. He laughed with Andy and sometimes at him.

After Andy went home Charlie would sit in his rocking chair, newspaper on his lap and carve on the horse until it was time to retire. He went to bed happy and slept better than he had in years. Charlie thought this must be what it is like to have a son. It was wonderful.

XI

Andy's dad hadn't felt good for a week. Mom said she thought he'd pulled a muscle or hurt his back while doing the heavy lifting the farm work demanded. He said he hadn't, but whatever was wrong it sometimes made his arm go numb. He complained that he felt weak and tired all the time. Andy had to take more responsibility. He had to do more of the chores and work in the fields every day with Dad.

There were numerous times when dark clouds gathered in the west, but there were no summer thunderstorms. The mid-summer dry spell made it necessary for the farmers to spend more time than usual in the fields tending to irrigation water. Charlie was no exception. It seemed like he was constantly changing water on one field or the other.

Dad wasn't feeling better, and Andy, at his mother's insistence, helped his father irrigate. In addition to tending the stream of irrigation water during the day, it was often necessary to redirect the water when irrigating the corn or grain at two or three o'clock in the morning. His mother got Andy out of bed to help his dad. After a week, Andy was tired all the time and usually fell into bed almost immediately after supper. Occasionally he would visit Charlie, but he would find himself dozing and have to excuse himself and go home. Charlie didn't mind because the extra work was exhausting him too.

The Parker household was a hive of activity during the first two weeks of August preparing for the wedding. Andy had to help clean the house although he couldn't understand why it had to be cleaned. The wedding and reception were to be held in the back yard and no one would be inside the house, but Mother wanted it scrubbed down completely.

Evenings were now spent addressing invitations and making lists of what had to be done. When he wasn't irrigating after evening chores, Andy escaped to Charlie's; but often Charlie was in the fields irrigating so they seldom saw each other.

One evening when Andy went over Charlie was there. They sat on the stoop in the evening shadows. Andy told Charlie all about the wedding plans.

"Will you come to the wedding?" Andy asked, "I'm sure Donna would like it if you did."

Charlie shook his head.

"Oh please come."

"Well, I'll think about it," Charlie said.

It had been so long since he had been to a social event that the thought scared him a little. The Parker's were relatives and if Andy wanted him to go then maybe he should, but what could he say to all those people? In a way he wanted to go. He realized he was nodding his head and saying, "We'll see."

Donna was surprised by Andy's request, but she said Charlie was certainly welcome. She gave Andy an invitation and he wrote Charlie's name on the envelope. He delivered it the following evening.

On Saturday Andy got a break from the heavy work schedule. Dad promised he could go to the matinee movie. Ray and Andy planned to ride their bicycles three miles north to Lewisburg. The movie theater was showing two serials and six cartoons. After he took Dad's and Charlie's herds to pasture, the plan was for Andy to go to the highway, travel north along the road for about a half mile to the unpaved lane. The lane went east from the highway and entered the town on the north side. It was the route on which Ray drove his herds to pasture. Andy was to meet Ray at the pasture gate at 8:15 and they would ride north to Lewisburg and have breakfast at Ray's aunt's house before going to the movie at eleven o'clock. Andy had enough money for the movie and a soda at the drugstore afterwards. It was a good plan and promised to be a fun day.

The morning was cool for a change. Andy hoped they got to Lewisburg before it got too hot. It wouldn't be bad riding home because it was pretty much downhill, but to get there they had to pedal up a slope almost all the way. It was murder if it was hot.

Andy turned off the highway onto the gravel lane and a bee hit his arm just below the elbow and stung him. It hurt like hell. The old canal ran alongside the lane so he stopped and put some mud from the canal bank on his arm. It helped a little but the pain was still there. He hoped it would go away and not swell and hurt and spoil his day. As he picked up his bicycle he noticed there were lots of bees buzzing around. There must be a new crop of weeds or alfalfa in bloom. Either that or he was in the flight line to a hive.

He mounted his two-wheeler and continued up the lane to the cutoff road that went past Ray's pasture. Just up the lane from the cutoff he saw a bicycle lying in the middle of the road. It was Ray's but he was nowhere in sight. Andy picked up the bike and leaned it against the fence by the side of the road, jumped on his bike and headed for Ray's pasture. There were still a lot of bees flying around. When he got there the cows were in the pasture and the gate was open, but Ray was nowhere in sight. Andy closed the gate and called out to Ray. There was no response.

Maybe he was kidnapped. The thought scared Andy and he jumped on his bike and pedaled toward town as fast as he could. When he got to where he parked Ray's bike, it was gone. Now Andy was really frightened. They had not only kidnapped Ray, they had stolen his bicycle. Andy zoomed into town, expecting at any moment to be grabbed by something or someone.

He went directly to Ray's house, but no one was home.

Poor Ray. They had always been friends. They were born a half a block from each other. Well not really. Ray was born in the hospital in the city, and Andy was born at home; but they lived close together all their lives.

The kids called them Mutt and Jeff because they were so different. Even though Ray was only three months older than Andy, he was a good five inches taller and had an olive complexion and dark straight hair. They always had fun at the old canal making up new games and playing in the water. Now he was gone.

Andy hurried home and told his mother what happened. She made some telephone calls but could find out nothing. She too was concerned. The waiting was awful.

The Harris automobile pulled into their driveway about eight o'clock that night. Ray's dad carried someone or something into the house. Was it Ray? Andy ran down the street to find out what happened to him. When he got there Ray's mother let him in and he saw Ray lying on the couch in the living room in obvious pain. His face was all swollen and red. Andy laughed. Ray looked like a tomato.

Ray's mother said it wasn't funny and pushed Andy into the kitchen. There she cleared up the mystery.

When Ray was taking his herd to pasture a truck passed him. It was a guy from Lewisburg transporting some hives of bees. The tailgate of the covered truck bed had bounced open. Ray was caught in the trail of angry bees streaming from the back of the passing truck. No matter which way he ran, the angry bees followed. He abandoned his bicycle and ran home through the fields, but not before he'd been stung about a hundred times all over his body.

After a frantic call from Ray's mom, his dad picked up Ray's bicycle on his way home. He worked in Lewisburg and hurried home to take Ray to the emergency room at the hospital. Ray had to have a bunch of shots. Andy knew it was serious, but when he pictured the whole incident in his mind, it was funny.

Ray was sick for a week, and he was mad as hell at Andy for laughing at his condition. Andy told Ray that God was just getting even with him for not owning up to his part in the old man Grant fiasco, and for not showing up to help him fix the fence. He never did tell Ray it was Charlie who did most of the fixing of the fence.

Andy was lounging on the porch swing when the black Plymouth pulled up in front of the house and Mike leapt out, jumped the fence and ran across the lawn. As soon as he saw Andy he put his finger to his lips signaling for Andy not to give away that he was home. He slugged Andy gingerly on the arm, smiled, patted him on the back and ran into the house. Andy ran after him.

For the next few minutes there was squealing and laughing, hugging and kissing and a few tears. Mike made it home a day early and his surprise was a huge success. It pleased Andy to see Donna so happy.

Mike only had a fourteen-day leave and they were to be married the day after he got home so there would be time for a honeymoon trip to Yellowstone Park before he went back to Georgia.

For two days the house was full of visiting relatives and friends. His aunt and uncle stayed at the house. Now he understood why Mom made him help clean the house.

Andy didn't mind that he had to give up his bed. Because Ray still didn't feel very good, he got to sleep outside at Johnny's house. He even got to eat there twice.

It was nice to have guests visiting and staying in the house because Mom made more desserts when there was company, and most desserts included ice cream.

Andy took the bag containing the quart of ice cream, said goodbye to Mr. Harris and left the service station. With a piece of string he secured the ice cream in one corner of the basket on the front of his bike so it wouldn't fall over on the way home. He always bought ice cream at the service station instead of the grocery store because Mr. Harris packed it in the container by hand, and he always put in so much the lid would hardly fold over to close. With the ice cream secure, Andy jumped on his bike and headed home.

As he passed the post office Mr. Otis came out of the door with a handful of letters and magazines. He waved to Andy and Andy waved back. He slowed down and made a wide turn in the street so as not to upset the ice cream. He wheeled up to Mr. Otis as the old farmer was mounting his horse.

"How're you doing, Andy?" Mr. Otis asked smiling down from his mount.

"Fine," Andy replied as he got off his bicycle. "Hey Mr. Otis, I've got something I want to show you." He fished the small piece of fabric from the money pocket of his jeans and carefully unwrapped his treasure. He handed the small arrowhead up to the old farmer.

Mr. Otis leaned down and took the bit of obsidian from him and inspected it. He held it up to the sun to see the light shine through it.

"This is nice Andy," he said, "Where did you find it?"

"I didn't find it. Charlie gave it to me."

The old farmer smiled and said, "So you got to see the collection after all?"

"Yes, and it's a great one."

"You and Charlie friends now?" Mr. Otis asked.

"Yep. I go over to his place a lot, and we have a great time."

"That's nice," Mr. Otis said, handing the arrowhead back to Andy.

Andy wrapped it and put it back into his pocket. "Well," he said, "I've got to get this ice cream home before it melts. See you at the wedding?"

"Sure will," the old farmer said. He nudged his horse with his heels. "See you later."

Andy waved and turned his bicycle and headed home.

Finally the day of the wedding arrived, and Andy worked with his dad to get things ready in the backyard. It was a hot day and one of the most humid of the year. Dad worried a storm might be coming in from the south. He said he hoped the late afternoon wedding and evening reception would be over before it hit the valley. Mom said if it rained they would move the wedding indoors. It would be hot and crowded but they would manage.

By noon all the tables and chairs borrowed from the church were set up and the trellis where the bride and groom would stand was in place. Flowers were carefully woven into the trellis latticework. Aunt Muriel was in charge of arranging the baskets of flowers that would be placed next to the trellis when the afternoon heat subsided.

Aunt Muriel was Andy's mom's sister. She was a rather short overweight woman with great energy. She laughed a lot. It was only natural to put her in charge of the flowers because she was a great organizer. Anytime there was a community function you could bet Aunt Muriel was right in the middle of things. Every 4th of July she not only helped clean and decorate the bandstand in the park, she cooked the hamburgers for everyone at the celebration. Dad said if they'd let her she would probably umpire the baseball game for the team. What Andy liked best about her was she had shelf after shelf of neat books in her house. When he went to visit there were always wonderful things to read and do.

They did chores early, much to the surprise of the cows, and by six o'clock everyone was dressing. Andy bathed at Aunt Muriel's because there was not enough hot water for everyone to bathe at home. He felt a little uncomfortable in Aunt Muriel's bathtub.

By six-thirty he was dressed in his suit and walking home. The heat was still stifling, and he was sweating from the tight collar, the tie and the wool jacket he wore. The sun occasionally broke through the heavy black clouds that were rolling into the valley from the southwest. It sure looked like it was going to be a doosie of a thunderstorm.

It never rained. The wind picked up from the south and blew across the west side of the valley, lifting clouds of dust from the dry farms on the foothills, but the wedding went off as planned. Donna looked beautiful.

She and Mike got tons of great gifts from the guests. Andy's job was to take the gifts from the people as they arrived and, making sure he didn't lose the accompanying card, take them to Aunt Muriel and her crew to be unwrapped and put on display on the long table next to the house with the other gifts. Andy felt important. No one said anything when he kept going back for more punch.

XII

Charlie finished his chores earlier than usual. He ate some dinner, bathed and shaved. The butterflies in his stomach increased as he thought about the evening ahead. From the window he could see the automobiles steadily filling the parking spaces in front of the Parkers' and their neighbor's houses. He watched as people dressed in their Sunday best and gifts in hand, chatted gaily as they walked down the street, through the front gate and disappeared into the backyard of the Parker house.

He took his gray-striped suit from the closet and hung it on the door. He had not worn the suit since Bessie's funeral. His hands shook as he buttoned the high-collared shirt, and it took him three tries to get the tie tied properly. It took him a couple of tries to get the vest buttoned correctly.

A gift. He had forgotten all about a gift. It did not occur to him until he saw the guests with their neatly wrapped and ribboned packages. In the second drawer of the sideboard was where Bessie kept her "good things," the things that were gifts to her but she had never used.

"They're too good for everyday," she said, "They are for special occasions." But the special occasions never came and so they were neatly folded and placed in the sideboard drawer.

Charlie carefully set each item on the sideboard until he came to a white linen tablecloth with embroidered edging. He laid it on the seat of the chair and carefully replaced the other articles back in the drawer. The closet in the spare bedroom was where Bessie kept all the boxes, wrapping paper and ribbon. She never threw anything away.

Everything was folded and put in a proper place for future use.

Bessie was beautiful on their wedding day. She wore her mother's wedding dress. Charlie, of course, was not allowed to see the dress before the wedding; and when he saw her coming down the aisle of the church he was struck by her radiant image. The late afternoon sun through the church windows lit the dust in the air and the entire church was bathed in an amber glow. Bessie looked so pure, so innocent. He wanted to protect her always.

His big hands could hardly manage the wrapping paper and ribbon. Wrapping a package for him was more difficult than carving a wooden horse. He was certain if he hadn't found a ribbon already tied in a bow, he would never have completed the package. It took what seemed to him forever to finish, and he was perspiring when he was finally done. He held the package up for inspection. He hadn't done a very good job, but it would have to do.

Brushing the curtain aside for a clearer view, he looked out the front window. The crowd had increased and there were now cars in front of his house. His stomach churned and he wished Andy would come over and walk to the reception with him. Perhaps if he waited for a while Andy would notice he wasn't there and come to his aid. He waited but Andy did not come.

Taking the gift he slowly made his way out of the kitchen door. He could hear the laughter and talking as he shuffled toward the front gate. When he reached the gate he could not force himself to open it. He stood for a few minutes gazing toward the Parker home and then turned and slowly went back to the house. He placed the gift on top of the other items in the second drawer of the sideboard and, without turning on a light; he changed back into his overalls and sat heavily in his rocking chair. Staring straight ahead, he began rocking slowly back and forth.

"You should have gone to the wedding Charlie."

"I know Bessie, I know."

XIII

By ten o'clock the reception was over. The exhausted but happy bride and groom piled their luggage into the trunk and backseat of the highly decorated black Plymouth and drove off to the cheers of relatives and friends who stayed for the send-off.

The house buzzed with conversation and rang with laughter as the group packed up gifts, washed myriad cups and saucers and cleaned debris from the backyard. Andy crawled sleepily to his sanctuary behind the sofa. Tonight might be a good night to listen to the conversations of the adults. He knew when they told him to go to bed that they didn't want him in the room. He didn't hear anything. Within minutes of settling in his sanctuary he was asleep.

Andy was awakened abruptly by the sound of urgent voices. He had no idea how long he'd been asleep, but someone had moved him from behind the sofa while he slept, put him on it and covered him with a blanket.

"Hurry, please hurry. He's in terrible pain." Someone was yelling.

"He's unconscious. Where are they? Why don't they hurry?" It was Andy's mother and her voice was coming from the bedroom. She broke into hysterical sobs.

The ambulance arrived within minutes. They carried Dad out on a stretcher. Mother went to the hospital with him in the ambulance. Andy was sent to stay with Aunt Muriel.

Andy couldn't sleep. He sat with his chin in his hands, elbows on the kitchen table and stared at a glass of milk. Across the table Aunt Muriel slowly stirred her tepid cup of tea. They sat for what seemed like hours.

Neither spoke. Andy wondered what he would do if his dad died.

"Is Dad going to be all right?" Andy finally asked.

Aunt Muriel tapped the spoon a couple of times on the edge of her teacup and, after a lengthy pause in which she seemed to be searching for the right words, said, "I don't know Andy. We'll just have to wait and see."

Andy retreated into his thoughts. They sat in the dimly lit kitchen, neither willing to suggest going to bed because both knew that sleep was impossible.

The silence was broken by the sound of the telephone. It was Andy's mother. Aunt Muriel talked with her for some time, but Andy could not make much sense from the side of the conversation he heard because Aunt Muriel was doing more listening than talking. After what seemed like an hour she handed the receiver to Andy saying his mother wanted to talk to him.

His mother's voice was strong and calm. Andy was told his father's condition was stabilized and there was nothing to do now but wait and see what happened. Andy was told to call Fred Olsen to help him milk and do the chores. Since Andy was the only one who knew what had to be done, he would have to tell Fred the milking routine and how much grain was given to each cow. The responsibility for the farm was his until his father recovered.

The heart attack was serious. Vern would have to remain in the hospital for four to six weeks, and following that he could do no work for six months to a year. He would probably never be able to do the heavy farm work again.

The only possible way to save the farm was to hire someone to run it until Ned was discharged from the army. The family could petition to have him discharged early because of the circumstances and the family's need, but that couldn't happen until he was shipped home from his overseas tour of duty. Ned was due to come back to the states in a few weeks. Emma hoped the money earned from the sale of milk and what they had in savings would be enough to pay a hired man and provide for the family until Ned got home. She had no idea how they would deal with Vern's hospital bill.

Fred Olsen agreed to work the farm until Ned returned. Andy worked with Fred to acquaint him with the daily operation of the farm. He also helped Fred irrigate the fields and prepare for the grain harvest. It took all of Andy's time and energy. He was exhausted. He didn't have the time or the energy to go to Charlie's in the evening.

XIV

Since the night of the wedding reception Charlie sat in his rocking chair every evening until well past his normal bedtime. Tonight was no exception. Several times he got up and went into the living room, pulled aside the lace curtains and stared across the street at the Parker house. He heard about Vern Parker's heart attack, and he knew the boy was busy and shouldering more responsibility than a boy that age should have to bear; but he wished Andy would come for a visit.

He left the back porch light burning and a light in the kitchen. No one with an upstairs bedroom went to bed before ten o'clock after the canyon winds swept away the afternoon heat from the stifling rooms so he knew the boy must still be awake.

From time to time he saw Andy, sometimes arriving home from the fields on the wagon with the hired man or trudging up the path from the Parker's barnyard with bucket in hand.

With the harvest beginning, Charlie worked in the fields until late in the evening. He milked the cows earlier than usual to allow him to get to the fields by sunup. He did not see Andy when he took the herd to pasture in the morning and he was not there when the herd was brought home in the evening. He tried to muster the courage to go to the Parker house to give Andy his August wages, but he settled for taping an envelope containing the money on the post by the corral gate.

Charlie removed another sliver of wood from the neck of the wooden horse. The flowing hair of its mane was almost done. He brushed the shavings into the center of the newspaper that lay in his lap to keep from making a mess on the kitchen floor. The detail work on the horse was going very slowly because he found himself looking out the front window each time he heard a noise. He wasn't able to concentrate anymore. Charlie was lonely.

He remembered the first time he felt so alone. After Ben died, Charlie laid in the big iron bed in the upstairs bedroom. Sometimes, unconsciously, he would reach over to find Ben only to realize he was gone. He remembered how he often laid awake long into the night crying. His eyes clouded with tears as he again felt the despair and hopelessness that affected him so much as a child. He needed someone to talk to.

Maybe Andy was angry with him because he didn't go to the wedding. He tried but just couldn't face all those people.

The childhood loneliness went away when he fell in love with Bessie. She filled the emptiness for him. They didn't talk much during the last years before she died, but she was there. Now she too was gone. He remembered how difficult her death was for him to face. It was the first time in his adult life he could not control his emotions. He remembered how his eyes filled with tears whenever anything reminded him that he was alone and how he withdrew from friends and relatives because he could not control himself; a man doesn't act that way.

When relatives and neighbors tried to help him after Bessie's death, he found it difficult to talk to them without his voice betraying his feelings. He didn't want to be unmanly in front of them so he told them to leave him alone and they did. In time he regained control but there was no one left around him. He was alone and he accepted it. He expected nothing from anyone, and in turn he was not disappointed when he received nothing. He was fine and had not felt like crying for years. He needed no one until the boy came along and Charlie was caught off guard. With Andy he began to dream again, to need again. His big hand wiped at his deep-set eyes. They were filled with tears. He was acting unmanly.

"You should go visit the boy."

"I know Bessie, I know," Charlie murmured, "I can't."

"Let me get you something to drink. Would you like something to drink Charlie?"

"Not now Bessie, not now."

His reverie was broken by a cracking sound. Looking down he saw he had unconsciously squeezed the carved horse that lay in his lap and broken off the lower part of the left hind leg. Again his eye filled with tears as he remembered how he felt the day he broke Ben's horse.

If only the boy would come to see me, Charlie thought. *There is so much I want to say. No, I shouldn't be with him, not now, not when I am acting so unlike the way a man should act. The boy should not see me this way.*

He could repair the horse's broken leg and it would look almost like new, but why should he? Charlie couldn't face the boy. Maybe he would fix the horse later.

Charlie took the broken horse, wrapped it carefully in tissue paper and placed it in a drawer in the bureau in his bedroom. He drew the shades on the living room windows. He would learn to be alone again.

XV

Andy thought about Charlie a lot. When he finally got home from working in one of the fields with Fred Olsen, it was late; and by the time he finished chores and ate supper, it was dark outside and he was exhausted. Even though he was dead tired he always checked to see if there was a light on in Charlie's house, but every time he looked across the street the old man's window shades were drawn and the house was dark. Andy thought Charlie must be tired from the heavy work and long hours required to harvest his crops and that the old man was going to bed early just like Andy was.

He missed the good times he had with Charlie. He was just getting to know the old man. They had so much still to talk about. He really loved Charlie. He learned so much from him. Charlie knew lots of things that no one else even knew about, except Mr. Otis. Andy thought about going to visit Mr. Otis, but Andy was certain his wife wouldn't like that.

He could listen all night to Charlie's stories about the old days when he was a boy. Andy couldn't wait until the harvest was over and he was back in school. Once the farm was prepared for winter there would be less work. The chores would be more demanding because the cows would be kept in the barn, but he wouldn't have to work all day in the fields. When he got out of school he would have time to go see Charlie. He couldn't wait.

Donna and Mike returned from their honeymoon trip early. They spent a couple of days sightseeing before they arrived in Yellowstone. There was no way to contact them while they were traveling so a message was left at the hotel in Yellowstone Park where they were planning to stay. When they arrived at the hotel they got the message, stayed the night and got back in the car and drove home.

Donna offered to stay and let Mike go to Georgia alone. She said the least she could do was stay until Ned got home, but Andy's mom said Fred had things well in hand. While she was with Vern at the hospital, Andy could stay nights with Aunt Muriel. She said there was no reason why Donna shouldn't go with Mike since Vern was out of danger and everything was under control. Mike and Donna stayed three days and left with a reluctant and tearful farewell.

An early frost the second week of September turned the fields of sweet corn brown. The dried leaves were like sword blades. They slashed the arms and faces of those who had the unpleasant task of stripping the ears for shipment to the canning factory.

Once the sweet corn was harvested it was top priority for the farmers to get the sweet corn stalks and the field corn chopped into silage and in the silos before all of the moisture was lost. Dry silage was terrible fodder for cows.

The early frost foreshadowed a long and cold winter.

Dad came home from the hospital after a four-week stay. He was thin and looked very tired. His movements were slow and deliberate. Andy saw the look of fear in his eyes. He was certain his dad was going to die.

Vern spent most of the day in bed and became more and more grouchy with each passing day. His inability to help with the farm work made him increasingly agitated, the precise thing he was supposed to avoid.

Mom was in constant contact with the commander at the army base trying to find out when Ned would be Stateside. She was also trying to get everything in order to make certain he got the early discharge. Every few days she was calling or writing to someone. The commander would not tell her exactly when Ned would return to the United States. He said it would be within a few weeks but the precise date was classified. Vern swore at the delays and accused those in charge of gross incompetence.

Fred Olsen quit because Vern was continually accusing him of doing something the wrong way. After a lot of pleading by Emma, Fred agreed to stay on until Ned got home. The tension was high and constant, and Dad's voice was often very loud around the house. It was exactly the opposite of what the doctor ordered.

Andy would be going back to school in late September right after the last of the crops, with the exception of sugar beets, were harvested and stored, and the farm would be buttoned down for the impending winter.

Sugar beets were the last crop to be harvested and that would happen in October. Sugar beets were the biggest cash crop for the farmer. The beet crop even brought in more money than peas, but the work was much harder. School was always cancelled for the last two weeks of October for Beet Vacation. It took a lot of manual labor to harvest sugar beets. Dad didn't grow sugar beets anymore so Andy planned to get a job with one of the other farmers. Everybody could get a job if they wanted one.

Andy remembered the story Charlie told when they were looking at his arrowhead collection. The one about the sugar beet that had grown around the arrowhead with the piece of buckskin attached. This year during the beet harvest, he was going to look very closely at the beets and see if he could find an arrowhead too. He would love to be able to tell Charlie a story.

The beets were often so big they were more than Andy could handle. Topping the large beets was left to the grownups, but there were plenty of smaller beets for Andy to top. Part of the job was to help load the beets on the wagon. That was where Andy could see if there were any arrowheads.

The wagons carried the beets to the beet dump where they were loaded into coal cars and a train took them to the north end of the valley to the sugar factory.

Harvesting sugar beets paid good money but it was hard work. Andy couldn't wait to get to work. After paying for old man Grant's fence, he could certainly use the money

The grass in the pastures had stopped growing, and Andy wondered how much longer the cows could glean enough feed from the pastures to justify taking them.

After Dad's herd of cows separated from Charlie's herd and Andy had locked the corral gate, he caught up with Charlie's cows just as they turned into the lane leading to the old man's corral. Andy was surprised to see Charlie standing in the barnyard. He locked the gate behind the cows and crossed to where Charlie stood leaning on the broken handled pitchfork. At his approach the old man lowered his head and pushed hay back into the manger.

"Hi," Andy said cheerfully, "I haven't seen you for a long time."

"You won't need to drive the cows anymore. The grass is gone and they're coming home hungry. Here's your pay," Charlie said. He fished a crumpled envelope from his back pocket and handed it to Andy.

"Thanks. Hey, we got all through with the corn, and I don't have to work after chores tonight. Can I come over?" Andy asked.

"No," Charlie replied and started toward the house.

"How about tomorrow night?" Andy called after him.

"Better not." And with that the old man went into the coal shed to change his clothes.

Andy didn't know what to think. Was Charlie mad at him for some reason? What had he done? He looked at the envelope in his hand, pocketed it and slowly rode his bicycle home. He was troubled by what just occurred.

During the following week, Andy went to Charlie's house three times; but the house was dark and he got no answer when he knocked at the door. He did not understand what happened, but since it seemed Charlie didn't want to see him, he stopped going over to the old man's house. Andy did not stop thinking about him. Whenever he saw Charlie in his yard Andy waved, but Charlie never responded.

Andy sometimes found himself kneeling on the sofa, just like when he was a little kid, looking out the living room window at Charlie's house. He was so sad about losing Charlie's friendship that he would often find himself crying. He didn't know what to do.

Dad told him to mow the lawn and trim the tall grass growing along the front yard fence for one last time before winter. The nights were cold but it still felt like summer during the day. This year the days were hot for September.

On Saturday morning Andy got up early to finish the task before it got hot. He didn't make it. By the time Andy was half way through the mowing, it was hot. He sat on the porch steps with a glass of cold lemonade resting before tackling the lawn west of the house.

Mr. Otis came down the street on his old roan horse, shovel over his shoulder. He was obviously going out to change the irrigation water in some field north of town, although Andy couldn't imagine what he would be irrigating so late in the season. Andy ran out to the gate to say hello to him. He climbed onto the gatepost and was waiting when the old farmer reined his horse next to the gate.

"How are you doing, Andy?"

"Fine Mr. Otis," Andy said, "Are you going out to your north field?"

"Yes, I've got a stream of water to tend to. It's so dry you have to irrigate before you can plow."

"Want some lemonade?"

"Ah, no thanks Andy," Mr. Otis replied, "I'm not much for sweet things. Say Andy, how's Charlie?"

"All right I guess. I don't see him anymore."

"Why? What happened?"

"I don't know," Andy said, "He doesn't seem to want me around."

"That's too bad," Mr. Otis said as he looked toward the old man's house.

"Yeah."

"Well I've got to get out to that irrigation water. I hope you and Charlie get things worked out," Mr. Otis said as he nudged his horse.

"Yeah, me too," Andy said. "See you later Mr. Otis."

Andy sat on the gatepost and watched the old farmer ride down the street. As he finished mowing the lawn, Andy's thoughts were on Charlie. Andy was lonely.

To fill the evenings since he was not spending them at Charlie's, Andy began drawing again. He used to draw a lot and he really liked drawing. Everyone in school said he was the best artist in his class, but that didn't mean much since none of the other kids could draw at all. His teacher said she liked his drawing too. After dinner and after he finished his homework Andy would draw, sometimes until bedtime. He thought that maybe someday he would go to a school and become an artist. He liked to draw animals and nature scenes best, but he was always finding something new to interest him.

When Andy arrived home from his first day back to school, he saw the automobiles in front of his house as he rode down the street and wondered if his mother was having her bridge club today. She hadn't said anything to him about it, and he hadn't noticed any special preparations being made that morning. There were always good things to eat after one of her bridge club meetings. He liked most everything except for the Jell-O salads; he didn't care much for them.

When he entered the back door he knew something was wrong. The doctor was there and Andy's mother was crying. Andy's heart leapt into his throat. Something had happened to his dad. He was dead. Andy ran to the door of the sickroom, but the doctor stopped him and told him to be quiet, his dad was sleeping.

If Dad is all right then what happened?

Andy slipped into the living room where his mother and a half-dozen friends and relatives sat quietly. His mother held out her arms to him and began crying again. Tears welled up in Andy's eyes. He knew his worst fear had happened.

"Ned is dead," Emma said simply as she tried to hold back her tears. "The ship he was on was attacked and sunk. Two army officers came to the door with the news and a telegram about an hour ago."

Andy sat stunned. It had happened. The worst thing in the world had happened. He cried some, but not for too long. He had cried for Ned a lot of nights.

In the days that followed he felt guilty about not crying more. It wasn't until weeks later when he was lying in bed thinking about Ned that he broke into uncontrollable sobs. After an hour of being comforted by his mother, he fell asleep. Things seemed better after that.

Ned's body was never recovered so a memorial service was held for him. The doctor made Dad go to the service in a wheelchair. He cussed and swore but the doctor was firm. After much coaxing by Emma, he reluctantly agreed. At the service Emma was given an American flag by the military guard and a small banner with a star in the center to hang in the front window to let people know those who lived in the house lost someone to the war.

Donna got home three days after the news about Ned was received, but Mike couldn't get a leave to come home. After the crying and comforting there was serious discussion and argument about the future of the farm.

Telephone calls were made to Mike. Vern tried to convince him to return when he was discharged from the army and take over the farm. Mike and Donna planned to stay in the east after he got out of the service, and no amount of talking would change their minds. Donna liked her new life and didn't want to spend the rest of her life in a small town. Vern was furious and called her ungrateful and accused her of destroying everything he'd spent his entire life building so he would have something to leave to his children.

Donna, who was as stubborn as Vern, packed her suitcases and left right after the memorial service, two days before she was scheduled to leave. It would be a long time before Andy would see her again.

Fred said he did not want to stay on and run the farm on a share basis. It was finally decided that since Vern couldn't do all the work the farm required and Andy was too young to take over, the land and most of the animals would be sold.

The cows were sold immediately because they were dry or had just calved. It was easier to sell them to farmers who knew they would have cows that would produce throughout the winter months. The cows that had calved were sold with the calf as part of the sale price.

Within a week all the cows, except the one they kept to supply milk for the family, were gone; and Andy's chores were reduced to feeding the chickens, the one calf that was not sold and the pig being fattened for spring slaughter. Dad milked the cow when he could. When he was too sick, Andy milked her.

A man who owned a farm down by the river bottom bought the team of horses, and the remaining cattle were sent to auction.

The farmer's co-op agreed to buy the harvested grain and find a buyer for the hay and silage they would not use now that there was only one cow and calf to feed. Most of the life was gone from the farm before the first snowfall.

XVI

Winter came early. Snow capped the tops of the mountains surrounding the valley by mid-October. The autumn leaves were vivid reds and golds and hadn't begun to fall from the trees when the first winter storms blew into the valley. The apples and sugar beets were harvested in the snow. With all the cold and snow to cope with during the sugar beet harvest, Andy forgot to look for arrowheads.

Pumpkins were capped with berets of white velvet before any of them had smiling Halloween faces. With the harvest moon came temperatures well below freezing. Children with boots and heavy coats over their costumes trudged through the drifted snow to collect the bounty of the season.

On Halloween night the town was quiet early and few tricks were played on the expectant citizens. Somewhere in the blanket of white, sleigh bells jingled as a lone horse carried somebody home from a Halloween party. It seemed more like Christmas than the end of October.

By Thanksgiving there was three feet of snow on the valley floor and much more in the mountains. From the first week of December until after the groundhog emerged from his hole in February and saw his shadow, the valley was shrouded in fog. Smoke from the coal and wood fires that were kept stoked day and night hung about the rooftops. The world was gray. The days seemed to crawl past, and by Christmas everyone was tired of winter.

Andy got a great idea. He would do a drawing as a Christmas present for Charlie. Maybe Charlie would like it and ask Andy to come for a visit.

He had been drawing pictures of cows, and they were pretty good. He decided to try and draw some of Charlie's cows and his lane with the cows going down the lane. He thought he could remember the markings on five of the cows. They were distinct and he knew Charlie would recognize which ones they were. He did several drawings before he got one that he liked. He decided that was the one that would be Charlie's Christmas present.

It was a strange Christmas for Andy without Donna and Ned to share it with him. Dad's attitude was worse than it had ever been. When Donna telephoned on Christmas Eve to wish everyone a Merry Christmas, he refused to talk to her, and that really put a damper on the holiday spirit.

Andy took his drawing and wrapped it in green paper and attached a ribbon. On Christmas morning Andy waited until he was sure Charlie was finished with the morning chores and took the gift across the street. He knocked on the door for a long time but there was no answer. He left the gift leaning against the kitchen door where he knew Charlie would find it.

Aunt Muriel invited the family over to her house for Christmas dinner because her entire family was coming home for the holidays. But Dad didn't want to go so Andy and his parents sat down to a quiet and somber Christmas dinner.

Christmas came and went without much joy. It seemed like more of a reminder of how much winter was still ahead than it did a holiday.

In early January the temperature fell to below zero and remained there for weeks. Because the sun couldn't dissipate the fog, the tree branches and power lines swelled with the accumulation of frost. Andy knew that when the fog lifted the valley would be a wonderland. The frosted poplar trees were shining giants that disappeared upward into the gray mist. It never got very light during the day. Morning and evening chores were done in the dark. It seemed as though the sun had given up trying to burn through the heavy blanket of fog, and everyone became short-tempered and depressed.

It was also depressing to see the deer suffer so much. By January they ran out of food on their winter range. They were forced by the heavy snow to come down into the valley to forage. As food grew more and more scarce, they moved into town to the farmer's haystacks.

Andy's family kept a small haystack to feed their cow and calf, and he saw tracks around it where deer had fed during the night. He saw only tracks because most of the deer moved to the edge of town when the farmers went to the barnyards to do chores in the morning.

The hay was not a good source of food for the deer. Even though they ate a lot of it, they couldn't digest the alfalfa so they got weaker.

By mid-January the deer were digging in the snow under the apple trees trying to find the rotting apples and leaves. They no longer left town during the day. They were so weak they just stayed in the calf pastures under the apple trees.

The deer were easy prey for dogs that roamed free in the town. Many deer were killed from attacks or from being chased into the barbed wire fences. The deer got weaker and many died of starvation or froze to death in the pastures. The town sent a sled around every other day to pick up the carcasses.

The townspeople were concerned for the future of the herd. The older people, who remembered that the deer were gone for so many years, wanted to save them. Andy didn't hear how the word spread, but farmers began locking their dogs in their barns to keep them from chasing deer. A group of men found the dogs that roamed free in the town and they were caught and confined or destroyed.

Andy remembered the stories Charlie told about the deer being hunted to extinction, and about their migration back into the mountains surrounding the valley in the 1920s. All the things Charlie told him were true. Andy wondered if the old man liked the drawing he left for him. He really missed Charlie.

Andy had no idea how many deer died, but the number was high. He would sit by the kitchen window in the evening with the lights out and watch the starving animals in the calf pasture in their vain search for food.

For a while Andy put out apples and some grain for the deer, but Dad told him he couldn't keep doing it all winter. Besides, the amount he was giving them was not enough for them to survive the winter. Dad said that all Andy was doing was prolonging their agony so he stopped. After a while he couldn't stand to watch the deer and wished they would die.

In the barns, the moisture from the animal's bodies and breath crystallized on the freezing cold concrete walls and on the windows. Shimmering walls of ice surrounded the animals huddled in the tightly closed barns.

Work for the farmers increased as hay had to be carried from the stacks by the corrals into the barns where the cattle were kept during the cold spell. Calves were brought from their sheds into the barn. The job of feeding the animals and cleaning the barns became an almost continuous one.

Andy got frostbite on his fingers when his hand, damp from milking the cow, stuck to a frozen faucet by the corral. He was attempting to get water for the chickens. By the time his mother came with a pail of hot water and freed his fingers, they were numb and frostbitten. Throughout the winter Andy was careful not to let the hand get cold. If it did, it was very painful.

From the window in the living room Andy could barely make out the silhouette of Charlie's house through the dense fog. He could not see the windows clearly, and there never seemed to be a light burning. On occasion he saw a shape emerge from the house and disappear down the path to the barnyard.

Andy heard stories told by the men at the service station about the really bad winters in the old days when the valley was first settled. They said the snowdrifts were higher than the eaves of the houses. Their stories, however, conflicted with the reports on the radio. The radio announcer reported that, according to official records, this was the worst winter in the history of the valley. The men said the worst winters were before records were kept.

Many of the stories Andy heard were just retellings of the stories Charlie had told him. Charlie told them better.

One morning in mid-February the sun burst through. The fog lifted and the wonderland Andy had waited so long to see sparkled in the crisp morning air. It was glorious. The frost had built up on the tree branches to the point that each twig appeared to be over an inch in diameter. Throughout the morning the heat from the sun loosened the frost and a shower of glittering crystals fluttered to the ground.

Even the power lines were heavy with the accumulated frost, and for a few morning hours the entire town appeared to have been flocked. The encrusted poplar trees were like giant inverted icicles that shot upward into the clear blue sky. Andy wished he had a camera to record the spectacle.

Spirits lifted and people smiled again. An air of optimism seemed to fill the town. Even Dad, who was finally up and around a lot more of the time and anxious to get back to work, had a more positive attitude.

As anxious as Vern was to get to work, the doctor would not allow it. If Vern disobeyed the doctor's orders it was at his own risk, and if anything happened to him the doctor would make it known it was Vern's fault. After much cussing and arguing, Vern finally agreed to seek a job in the city. He found employment as a bookkeeper in a dry goods store owned by a boyhood friend.

The routine in the Parker house changed because Vern didn't have to be at work until nine o'clock in the morning. Andy could milk the cow and do the other chores in less than an hour. Breakfast was now served at eight o'clock; that allowed Dad time to eat and to still have time to catch the streetcar for the twenty-minute ride to the city.

Andy was allowed to sleep until six-thirty. He thought it was great not to have to get up at five o'clock. Andy was glad to be rid of the farm work.

The extended stay in the hospital had put a strain on the family's finances. It took most of the money from the sale of the animals to pay the bills. The cost of living for the months when Vern couldn't work had taken what little they had in savings and put them in debt.

There would be money when the land was sold, but there was still no buyer for the acreage. To help the family, Andy got a job stocking shelves at the grocery store. He worked from the time school let out until six o'clock. Then he went home to do his chores. But the job didn't last very long because Mr. Wells, the grocer, said Andy was too small to handle the cases of canned goods. He said he was sorry, but he had to hire someone who could do the heavy lifting. Andy found himself with nothing to do but a few chores.

Evenings, after chores and dinner, were boring for Andy. He would draw sometimes but he would always think about going to Charlie's.

The spring run-off from the snow in the mountains normally began in May, and the streams flowing into the valley gradually rose and crested in late June, but in early April warm winds blew up from the south and the mountain snows began melting. The valley snow melted and revealed the dead brownish-gray of the valley floor within two weeks. The leaves whipped from tree branches by the early winter storms and buried by the white shroud all winter lay crushed and matted on the dormant lawns.

By mid-April the snow was gone. The water from the rapid snowmelt high in the canyons crashed down the mountainsides into streams that flowed into swollen rivers. The rivers rushed from the canyons, spilled over their banks and washed everything in their path into a muddy lake in the river bottoms, flooding the center of the valley.

The head gates of irrigation canals were opened and ran at full capacity to alleviate the overflowing river and to protect the city from extensive flooding.

Tables from picnic areas in the canyon washed downstream and collected like driftwood along the edges of the reservoirs. They were rescued by forest rangers and carried to high ground until the crisis passed.

117

To complicate the problem the spring winds began in earnest. They blew directly from the east. It was a terrible spring. The topsoil in the fields dried too fast and crusted. Farmers used harrows and disks to break up the concrete hard crust, but that just created large clods all over the surface of the fields. With an abundance of irrigation water, some farmers irrigated their fields to break up the clods before planting and to get enough moisture in the soil for seeds to germinate.

The wind also raised havoc in town. The Perry's barn, which was emptied of hay during the long winter, lost its roof to the gusting wind. It was literally peeled off the walls in two large sections and deposited across the middle of the road more than a hundred feet away.

But by far the biggest problem was with the poplar trees. They fell like soldiers in battle. Some split as the wind tore away huge limbs. Other trees were uprooted as well.

One of the giants in front of Ray's house was downed. The enormous roots held fast to the chunk of earth beneath it, and as it fell it tore up sections of the sidewalk and crushed two lengths of the picket fence.

Andy lay in bed listening to the wind pound against the windowpane. It would subside and then a gust would hit with such force the window would rattle and the house tremble from the power of the blow.

Andy's mother hated the spring wind. She was afraid one of the old trees would blow onto the house.

The wind had blown for three days and showed no sign of letting up. It would subside a little during the day, but not much, and then pick up force at night.

After school was fun because Andy could open his coat like a sail and run home almost effortlessly, but in the morning with the wind hitting him directly in the face Andy wasn't sure if he'd make it to school. Occasionally he would have to take shelter behind one of the trees that remained standing and catch his breath before confronting the gale again.

A gust of wind pounded the window and jarred Andy into awareness. It was late and the third time tonight the pounding of the wind woke him up. He lay listening to the tempest rage outside. Suddenly there was a terrible cracking sound, a loud pop and a tremendous crash. Andy knew somewhere nearby another of the battered giants became a victim of the onslaught.

XVII

Charlie sat in the kitchen with a blanket wrapped around his legs. It was the same almost every night all through the dark winter months. He sat in his rocking chair every evening, but he no longer stayed up past his bedtime.

Winter was always difficult, but this one was worse than usual. He often came into the house after the evening chores so exhausted he would have to rest before cooking his evening meal.

With the cattle always in the barn, it took extra time after each milking to feed them and clean the barn. There was a time when he could work all day and not feel the effects, but now it was hard for him to even get out of bed in the morning.

He tried not to think of the boy anymore. When the images and thoughts came, he did his best to push them out of his mind. It was too painful to be constantly reminded of how lonely he was.

The animals that depended on him demanded his time. He kept busy and tried not to think too much. Each morning he would force himself to get up and continue the seemingly endless routine.

His eyes filled with tears when he sat in his chair in the shadows of the kitchen and listened to the timid knocking on his door. It was difficult not to respond, but he did not move until long after the creaking sound of the front gate closing had faded. He found the green package leaning against the kitchen door.

It was Christmas. He knew the holiday was at hand, but to Charlie Christmas was like any other day. They used to celebrate the holidays. Charlie surprised Bessie with a tall fir Christmas tree on their first

Christmas together in the new house. He told her he was going to the vinery to get pea silage for the cattle, but instead he took the sleigh and drove to the foothills. That was a hard winter too. He had to leave the sleigh and trudge through waist-deep snow for a good half mile to the side canyon where the firs grew. When he got home he was tired and wet, but it was worth it to see the look on Bessie's face.

They had no Christmas decorations so they made them. They strung popcorn and cranberries on long strings and made candleholders out of old thread spools. Charlie made a star for the top of the tree out of cardboard covered with tinfoil, and Bessie made and decorated gingerbread cookies in a variety of ornament shapes. When they finished, the tree looked festive.

They almost burned down the tree and the house that year because they sat too long looking at it one evening and the candles burned too low. From then on every year Bessie made him put a bucket of water in the closet next to the tree.

Charlie never hung the picture left on his porch. He unwrapped it, looked at it for a while and then put it back in the green paper, taped it closed and put it in the trunk.

He considered repairing the carved horse and giving it to the boy but decided against it. He knew if he were to see the boy tears would flow, and he couldn't let the boy see him like that. He didn't understand why his emotions were so close to the surface now. It was never that way in the past. He was a man. He didn't cry.

He remembered Ben. Christmas was always fun when Ben was alive. They had wonderful times on Christmas morning. He was so proud when he surprised Ben with a stocking cap. He planned all fall for the surprise. He carried wood and did odd jobs for his aunt to get her to knit it for him. Ben was surprised and very happy with the gift.

Charlie couldn't remember exactly when they stopped having a tree at Christmas. Bessie just seemed to lose interest and told him it was too much bother. Somewhere in the closet in the spare bedroom or in the cellar was a box with all the ornaments they collected over the years.

Charlie felt the winter cold like never before. His hands, calloused and toughened by years of doing the same tasks, seemed to be constantly cold, and the joints of his fingers were stiff and painful.

He bought a new pair of gloves, but it didn't help. He tore the skin on the palm of his hand one morning when he jerked it off the barnyard faucet when it stuck to it during the cold spell in January. It neither healed nor worsened. The sore would appear to be healing only to have the scab rub off while he was milking the cows.

"You've got to put some salve on that or it will get infected."

"I know Bessie, I know. I'll get some next time I go to the store," he said.

His back ached all the time now. It was probably strained when he slipped and fell while carrying a water-soaked frozen bale from the shed to the barn in January. It just never seemed to get better.

Caught up with the pressures of the heavy winter, Charlie had been able to think less about the boy. On a few nights when he sat in his rocking chair before going to bed, the memories came back of the nights they talked for so long about the arrowhead collection and nights he spent telling the boy stories. His eyes would fill with tears, and he would realize what was happening and quickly try to occupy his mind by doing some household chore or going to bed.

Every time the image of the boy covered from head to foot in mud came back to him, he smiled.

Charlie was jarred back to reality by the clatter of the windowpane as a gust of wind shook the house. The spring winds seemed stronger each year. This year they were strong enough to do considerable damage to both buildings and trees. Because the poplar trees were old and rotting, he worried about the winds.

The house creaked under the onslaught of the heavy wind gusts.

Charlie moved the blanket aside, got up and went to the kitchen stove. The embers were still glowing, so he threw in a lump of coal and stirred them with a poker to allow them more air. Within a minute the flames danced over the added fuel. He left the damper open so the smoke would go up the chimney and not into the room, and then he put the stove lid on the far side of the stove. The flames lit up the kitchen walls and cast dancing shadows on the wallpaper. The flame brightened and the frenzied shadows leaped higher with each gust of wind.

Charlie went to the kitchen window, pulled back the curtains and looked into the yard. It was strewn with small branches that had been ripped from the poplar trees. The branches blown down earlier in the day were most likely blown up against the door of the coal shed or against the foundation of the house.

He looked down the path toward the barnyard to make certain the barn was still standing. The weatherworn shingles shimmered in the moonlight. He was thankful that they were still intact. He didn't know what he would do if the shingles or the barn roof blew off. He didn't have money to have it repaired.

A gust of wind rattled the kitchen windows and he reacted with a start. He wondered when it would stop. The wind had been blowing for days. Each morning he expected to find the wind had died down, but it continued.

Charlie felt old. He was tired and sore and needed the warmth of a spring day to help him recover his strength.

"What's the use of trying to go on anymore?" Charlie thought, *"What difference does it make?"*

He knew most people thought he was too old to be farming, but up until this past year he hadn't felt much different than he had for the last forty years. He could lift sacks of grain with the best of them. At harvest time he got his crops in as quickly as any of the other farmers. He enjoyed farming. There was no reason to quit. Besides, what would he do if he stopped farming?

Recently, however, during the long gray days of winter, he noticed a shortness of breath, and in the morning when he got up there was stiffness in his legs and his shoulders hurt more each day. During the day while he worked the muscles would loosen and the pain would subside a little, but in the evenings when he sat in his chair the pain returned to his shoulders and hands.

He replaced the lid over the open fire, sat down and pulled the blanket across his knees. He was tired during the day, but it was probably because he didn't sleep well. He wished he could stop the pain. He shifted in the chair to find a comfortable position where the pain was bearable, but it was not possible. Aspirin no longer eased the pain, and Charlie thought maybe he should go to the doctor and try some new drug, but he didn't trust doctors. Bessie hadn't trusted doctors either.

"There are plenty of good home remedies," she said, "My mother had remedies that cured almost anything. Let me make one for you to ease the pain."

"No. It's all a bunch of malarkey."

"It certainly is not," Bessie said, "It's in the Bible. There are all sorts of medicines that are found in plants. Do you think the Lord would put us here on earth without ways to cure illness and disease?"

Charlie laughed.

"Besides, if you eat the proper things there is no reason why you should get sick in the first place."

He laughed again, and the more he laughed at her the more she argued her position.

Most of the townspeople swore by the old medicine. They even believed in the signs for planting and harvesting. Corn should not be planted until the snow left the crest of Saddle Mountain east of town. Charlie kept track of how well the signs worked when he was starting to farm, and they didn't work as far as he could tell. Still the townspeople blamed themselves if something didn't turn out according to the signs, and the next year he would hear some farmer say that according to the signs it was time to plant.

A gust of wind rattled the kitchen window and jolted Charlie back to reality. He moved and pain shot through him. He didn't know how long he had been dozing, or if he was asleep at all. The room was cold. The fire had burned down so he put another lump of coal on the embers and went through the routine of stoking the fire.

He opened the oven door to let heat into the room. The rush of warm air felt good on his stiff fingers. He got a one-inch stack of folded newspapers and laid them on the open oven door. He wrapped the blanket around his shoulders and sat on the oven door. The warm air on his back soothed the pain. He took the blanket from his shoulders and wrapped it around his legs and warmed his hands between his knees. As the pain eased he began to relax; he forgot about the wind and cold outside.

"One of these days you're going to break that door right off the stove," Bessie chided, "and then what will we do?"

"This stove is cast iron and steel," Charlie said, "It's not going to break."

"Since you've been sitting on it the door is much looser, and it doesn't shut tight any more."

"It has always been like this, and if it doesn't shut tight then it's because you're not latching the latch properly," Charlie said, not moving from the door.

"You'll see. You'll see. Don't say I didn't warn you," Bessie said, and she stormed off into the living room.

Charlie bought the stove shortly after they were married, and he liked to sit on the oven door. He sat on it when he lit the fire on cold winter mornings. It was a good place to sit while putting on shoes because the heat took the chill out of the cold kitchen air. Besides, he had always done it at home when he was growing up, and he never broke a door; it was sturdy as the day he first sat on it.

The pattern on the linoleum in front of the stove was almost worn away. He remembered installing it and the morning Bessie dropped a frying pan and put the first mark in it. Some day he would have to replace the linoleum, and it would have to be tan because Bessie liked tan linoleum best. When Muriel put light green flooring in her house Bessie told him how awful it was. She would never put anything but tan in her kitchen.

He heard a tremendous crack, a loud pop and glass shattered in the living room. Charlie leapt to his feet, his heart pounding he ran to the door. The lace curtains on the east living room window were shredded, and the green blind was ripped from the roller and lay beneath the branches. The shredded curtain flapped in the gusting wind. The glass scattered across the floor reflected the moonlight. A large branch stuck through the shattered window.

He turned on the chandelier. The room was filled with branches and pieces of glass were everywhere. Pictures were toppled off the sideboard, and a branch had torn the green velvet on the chair.

Charlie went back to the kitchen. He closed the living room door to stop the wind from gusting through the house. From the back stoop he saw that his east poplar tree was down. The roots had clung to the soil and lifted a huge ball of earth when it fell. Bared roots stretched into the air. Most of the fence was destroyed. Splinters of white pickets were strewn across the front lawn. It was the top of the giant poplar tree that hit the side of the house and crashed through the window. From his vantage point Charlie had no idea how much damage the fallen tree did to the house in addition to the broken window.

There was nothing to do but wait until morning to assess the damage, and wait until the winds died down to clean up the mess.

Charlie spent the remainder of the night in his rocking chair. He slept little. Because the windbreak provided by the east tree was gone, the other tree could blow over as well, and it could do even more damage to the house.

"What are you going to do about that mess? The living room is destroyed. You've got to clean it up."

"I know Bessie, I know," he said quietly, *"But I'll have to do it tomorrow. I'm very tired."*

"I warned you this would happen. I told you to cut them down long ago. I warned you."

"I know. I know," the old man muttered. He closed his eyes and leaned back in his chair.

The wind kept up its fury all night.

126

XVIII

The winds stopped and it rained. It was wet and cloudy for the remainder of the week, and then the sky cleared. The sun emerged and so did all the townspeople to survey the devastation.

The damage caused by the downed poplar trees was extensive. After surveying the devastation the community leaders voted in an emergency town meeting to remove all of the remaining poplar trees.

The project was in full swing in less than two weeks after the winds stopped and before the clean up of the debris was complete. A logging company was hired, and a crew equipped with saws, axes, tractors with loaders and a fleet of trucks descended on the wounded giants. Half of the people in town volunteered to help with the cleanup.

Throughout the school day Andy heard the constant noise as the army of workers advanced through the town. Most of the school-age boys, including Andy, worked after school and on Saturdays. They followed the destructive march with rakes and wagons, and they cleaned up the small branches and wood chips left by the armed force that systematically went up one street and down the next removing all of the towering sentinels.

Within three weeks they were gone, and the planting of the red maples, the shade tree selected to replace the poplars, began. Flatbed trucks unloaded enough maple saplings in five-gallon cans to plant a new tree every forty feet along the front of each yard. The Parkers' maples were sitting next to the porch when Andy got home from school on Wednesday. It took two evenings for Andy to dig the holes. With his mother's help and his father's supervision, the trees were planted.

They were scrawny and four to five feet tall. Andy wondered how many years it would be before they would be tall enough to provide good shade.

On Saturday Andy planned to get up early and finish any jobs his mother might have on her list for him to do. He wanted to be done in time to go to Lewisburg with Ray to see the matinee movie.

Mom woke him at seven-thirty. He only laid in bed for about fifteen minutes before he was up and dressing.

"Mom," he called from the bedroom door, "where are my jeans?"

"I washed them this morning, Andy," she called from the kitchen, "Get a clean pair from the closet."

He hated to put on a clean pair of pants just to do work. Why hadn't she waited until after he'd finished his chores? He put on the old pair of jeans with the holes in the knees and saved his tan corduroy pants for the trip to Lewisburg.

His mother didn't have many jobs for him; he finished them and his breakfast by nine o'clock.

With his mother's approval he washed up and went upstairs to change his clothes. He put on his tan corduroys and a pullover. He took the tobacco tin he used for a bank from his dresser drawer and took out enough money for the movie ticket and a treat afterwards. He got his wallet, pocketknife and other valuables from the table next to the bed where his mother had put them when she emptied the pockets of his jeans.

"Where's my arrowhead?"

It was not with his other valuables. Had his mother washed his pants with his good luck piece still in the pocket?

"Mom, where did you put my arrowhead?" he yelled from the bedroom door.

"What arrowhead?"

"My lucky arrowhead. The one that I always keep in the money pocket of my jeans."

There was no reply.

They looked everywhere. Andy found the piece of cloth he wrapped his treasure in stuck to the drain screen where the washer was emptied, but the arrowhead was nowhere to be found. His mother felt bad about the mistake. She normally checked all of Andy's pockets before washing, but somehow she missed his treasure.

Andy cried. His precious arrowhead was gone. He didn't enjoy the matinee.

The following Saturday it rained all day. The boys planned to go to another matinee, but it was raining too hard to make the bicycle trip so they decided to play Monopoly instead.

They called Paul but he wasn't home. Johnny had to help his dad and couldn't come over to Ray's until after lunch. They said they would wait for him. To kill time they laid out the game board and sorted the money and the deeds and set up the bank.

Ray's mom called to him from the kitchen and asked him to take the tea tray to his Grandma Harris's room. Andy followed. He helped Ray put the wedges of wood under the chair rockers to stabilize it. They put the board across the arms, and Ray sat the tray in front of the old woman. She often got out of her chair with the help of her cane, but she preferred to have tea in her chair rather than sitting at the table. She was sometimes very quiet, but today she was in a good mood and wanted to talk.

Andy was delighted. He hadn't heard her tell stories for a long time. The boys took the pillows from the small settee and settled comfortably on the rug in front of her.

"Whose boy are you?" the old lady asked.

"I'm Andy Parker. I live up the street," Andy replied.

"Oh, I remember the Parkers."

She carefully but somewhat shakily poured tea from the small pot into her cup and added three spoonfuls of sugar. Andy thought that was an awful lot of sugar for such a small cup.

Grandma Harris began talking about the Parker family and how she remembered when they arrived in town. She was living with her family in a dugout house over by the springs because none of the log houses that were being built on the town site were finished. Andy asked what a dugout house was and she said it was just a cave dug out of the sidehill. It provided shelter in a storm, but cooking and most of the living was done out of the cave. The dugout was only big enough for sleeping quarters, storage for the furniture they brought across the plains and for their food supply. As houses were completed, families moved into them and newly arriving families took over the dugouts until their homes were built.

The Parkers' arrived before anyone had moved out of a dugout, and there wasn't an embankment left that didn't already have a dugout carved into its side so the Parkers' lived in their wagon for more than a month.

She suddenly stopped talking about the Parkers', and after a long pause began talking about building the church house. She said that she worked with all the other kids gathering rocks of all sizes and shapes to be used in its construction. She then began to ramble, talking first about earning her place in heaven and then about someone named Metcalf whom she hated and hoped went to hell. The more she talked, the more agitated she became. Suddenly she shoved the tray off the board. It crashed on the floor at her feet. Mrs. Harris came running into the room. She and the boys picked up the pieces of shattered china and wiped up the spilled tea and sugar.

The old woman did not stop her chattering, and the boys were sent out of the room with the tray while Ray's mother tried to calm her down.

Andy thought that was a weird way to act, and Ray was embarrassed by what happened. Johnny arrived and they settled down for a long game of Monopoly. They had played for about an hour, and Andy had acquired Vermont Avenue, all of the railroads, Pennsylvania Avenue and Park Place. He had quite a bit of money and it seemed as if he might win this time.

Suddenly the door to the old woman's room opened with a bang, and she hobbled into the room mumbling to herself. She wore a black velvet, broad-brimmed hat with feather trim and a veil. She had a black brocade dolman cape over her housedress, but she still wore the cloth house slippers on her feet. She called to Ray's mother, yelling something about it was time for church. Mrs. Harris told her it was Saturday and there was no church today, but the old woman didn't believe her; and she yelled that Mrs. Harris was trying to keep her from church and out of heaven.

Andy and Johnny sat awed by the scene, but Ray quickly got up to help his mother. Mrs. Harris tried to get the old woman back into her room, but when she approached the old woman struck her on the side of the head with her cane. Ray and his mother finally subdued her and with one on each arm they led her back into her room. She continued the harangue, and Andy and Johnny heard her yelling even after the door was closed.

Within a few minutes Ray and his mother emerged from the room. Ray's mother was unhurt but crying. She went to the kitchen, and Andy heard her talking to someone on the telephone. Ray said he was sorry about what happened. Grandma Harris was getting worse all the time. She thought everyday was Sunday and always wanted to be taken to church.

Because she was getting so violent, the family had decided she would have to be put in the old folks home in the city where she could be watched all the time. Ray's father didn't want to do it because the house belonged to Grandma Harris, and he was concerned about what the townspeople would think if he had her put away. It had to be done because Ray's mother couldn't handle her anymore, and if they didn't do something the old woman was going to hurt someone or herself.

The game was called. None of the boys felt like playing after what happened so they packed away the game and Andy and Johnny went home.

What happened? She seemed all right when she was telling stories.

Andy wondered if this sort of thing happened to all old people. It was weird.

On Monday, Andy saw the Harris automobile pull out of the driveway. The old woman was in the back seat. She probably thought she was going to church because she wore the broad-brimmed hat and dolman cape. She smiled and waved to Andy as the automobile passed. That was the last time he saw the old woman alive.

Two weeks after Andy saw the Harris' car drive away with the old woman in the back seat, he was sitting on the step outside the kitchen door drawing. He heard his mother talking on the telephone with someone. When she hung up the telephone, she called Andy into the house. They sat down at the kitchen table.

"That was Ray's mother on the phone," she said. "Ray's great grandmother died in her sleep last night."

"I'm sorry," Andy said.

"She had a good long life. She was the last of the original pioneers that settled our town."

"I know," Andy said. "My favorite story was the one she told about her walking across the plains."

"She was quite a storyteller wasn't she?"

"Yeah. Was grandpa a pioneer?" Andy asked.

"No, he was born quite a few years after the town was settled," Emma said. "I guess the oldest people in town now, the last of the first generation born right after the pioneers got here, are Charlie and Bill Otis. There are a few more people from that generation still alive but, like your grandfather, they don't live here anymore."

"Where did they go?"

"Well, not everybody likes farming so those who didn't moved away. A lot of people prefer city life," Emma said. "When Charlie and Bill pass away, all early settlers will be gone."

Andy didn't want to think about that.

Because of his friendship with Ray, Andy's mother said he should go to the funeral. He did and it was sad. The preacher talked a lot about old Mrs. Harris being the last of the pioneers.

Mr. Otis was there, but Charlie wasn't.

After the funeral, lunch was served to the people who attended. Andy and Ray went outside and sat on the front steps. Ray just sat staring straight ahead.

"What are you thinking about?" Andy asked.

"Grandma Harris," Ray said. "I can't stop thinking about how much she changed. She wasn't like Grandma Harris when we took her to the city. She was like a different person."

"Yeah. I know."

"Are you still hanging around old Charlie?" Ray asked.

"No. The last time I saw him, he was acting different too."

"Why did you start going over to his place anyway?"

"Because he's a great old guy," Andy said. "I wish I was still going over to see him. He tells great stories."

"About what?"

"The old days. You know the same kind of stories your grandma told, and he's got the greatest arrowhead collection," Andy said. "I showed you the one he gave me. Didn't I?"

"Yeah it's a great one."

"It was until my mom lost it in the washer."

"When?"

"About a month ago."

"Do you think old Charlie would give you another?" Ray asked.

"I don't know. I don't think I'll get to see him again."

After supper Andy sat on the porch and looked across the street at Charlie's house. He wanted so much to be with him. Tears came to his eyes. He wiped them away and went into the house to draw.

XIX

Charlie held his large blue and white print handkerchief under the running water, turned off the tap and wrung out the handkerchief. He wiped the perspiration from his forehead and sat heavily on the bench by the coal shed letting the spring breeze blow across his fevered brow. The coolness of the wet cloth soothed him and the dizziness eased. He felt like a fool, nearly collapsing. What was wrong with him? He had not worked that hard and it was still morning sun.

He had hated seeing the logging company cut down the healthy poplar trees, but he knew he couldn't stop them. As much as he didn't like what they were doing, he was thankful the town had them haul away the trunk of the fallen poplar tree. They said they would be back to cut down his remaining tree. He protested but they said for him to take it to the mayor.

Charlie told the men to leave most of the limbs because he wanted them for firewood. He worked for three days to cut the large branches into sections small enough for him to load on his milk cart and stack behind the coal shed for splitting come winter. He shuddered at the thought of another winter. He needed help, but everyone was as busy as he was cleaning the debris from their yard.

There was still a lot of work to be done. All the small branches and leaves had to be cleaned up, and Charlie wasn't sure he had the energy to do it.

He felt as if his world was crumbling around him. The rigors of trying to take care of the cows through the winter had taken a lot out of him, and now he was having a hard time coping with the demanding spring farm work. The added work that the fallen tree cleanup and fence repair would require was the last straw. He didn't know if he could do it.

The exhaustion he felt every day after doing the routine chores bothered him. He felt old and useless. Soon spring would be fully upon him, and the pasture and lawn grass would grow and the crop would need planting and tending. How was he going to get all the work done? He couldn't afford to hire a man to help him. What would he do about taking the cows to pasture? He couldn't walk that far twice a day. He would have to ride one of the workhorses; there was no other way.

"You're working too hard," Bessie said from the kitchen doorway, "Come in and have a glass of lemonade."

Charlie rose and pocketed the wet handkerchief. His body ached as he slowly made his way into the kitchen.

"You're going to make yourself sick if you keep this up," Bessie chided, "and if you get sick, what am I going to do? I can't run the farm."

"I'll be all right, Bessie." Don't worry," Charlie muttered. He poured a glass of lemonade, set it on the table beside his rocking chair and sat down heavily.

Even though he tried to put them out of his mind, the images of Ben, or was it Andy, kept coming into his head. He remembered how Ben and he would sit on the bench by the coal shed and talk late into the summer evenings. They had some good times together. He smiled at the thought.

Charlie was awakened by the sound of axes chopping. The clock read seven-thirty. For the first time in his memory, he had overslept. He got out of bed and discovered he was dressed. Then he realized he'd finished the morning milking. Had he fallen asleep after breakfast? He couldn't remember going back to bed. No matter, he must get to work.

When he opened the kitchen door the sound of the axes, men's voices and trucks grew louder. From the front of the house he saw one of the large poplars in front of the Parker house fall, and a swarm of workmen descend upon it and begin ripping it apart. Charlie didn't want to watch what they were doing so he harnessed his team and went to the south field.

Charlie returned from the field in late afternoon to find his remaining poplar tree was down and most of it was gone. The old man's eyes filled with tears. Those bastards. How could they cut down his tree?

In the days that followed, Charlie watched as the trees disappeared from the horizon of the town. They were destroying part of his life. He remembered so well the planting, and he watched them throughout the years as they grew to maturity. He grew up with them and now they were gone. He shook his head. Inside he felt a great emptiness.

He came home from a day of harrowing the north field to find three five-gallon cans sitting next to his porch. Each contained a maple sapling. There was a note attached to one of the scrawny trees that had words and numbers on it. They were probably instructions for planting the trees to meet town regulations. Charlie did not plant the trees.

He lay on his bed. He had stopped perspiring and the pillow had absorbed the moisture. The pillowcase was cool from the evaporation and the room felt chilly. He rolled his head to the side and felt the coolness of the damp cloth on his cheek. His head still swam and the pain had not gone away. He lay on the bedspread with his soiled boots hanging over the edge of the bed. He still wore his overalls; Bessie didn't approve of that. He should have taken off his shoes and changed his clothes in the shed, but he couldn't do it. The pain was too strong and he was dizzy, but the pain had stopped. He must get up and change his clothes so he wouldn't soil the bedspread. He opened his eyes and pulled himself to a sitting position on the edge of the bed.

The bedroom door opened and a small figure stood silhouetted in the doorway.

"Is that you, Andy?" the old man whispered.

The smile was innocent and the laughter infectious, and Charlie smiled at the happy sound. But it wasn't Andy. It was Ben.

The cows mooed late into the morning. When the milkman noticed the full cans of milk had not been brought to the milk stand, he went to the barn to see if something was wrong with the old man. The cows had not been milked or fed.

He summoned the sheriff who went into the old man's house when he got no response to knocking on the door. Charlie was lying beside the bed. It appeared he had just slid from the bed onto the floor. There was no sign of a struggle. The doctor was sent for. He examined the body and signed the death certificate. The officials were efficient and by noon the old man's body was loaded into a hearse and taken to the city.

XX

When Andy got home from school at four o'clock, his mother sat him down at the kitchen table and told him about Charlie. Andy cried.

After he finished his chores Andy went across the street to Charlie's place. He sat on the bench by the coal shed where they sat so many evenings talking. He felt as if Charlie was sitting beside him, and his mind was flooded with memories, happy memories. When night fell, Andy went home.

He was sorry more people didn't attend the funeral. Besides Andy's parents, there were only the Otis's, several townspeople, a few of Charlie's distant relatives that Andy had never seen before, and the preacher.

Only about half of the church choir showed up to sing. The service was very short, and Andy thought the preacher didn't say very much. He kept saying how nobody knew the old man very well.

After the funeral Mr. Otis came up to Andy and put his arm around his shoulder. He smiled at Andy and said, "We know better, don't we?"

Andy started to cry and Mr. Otis led him out of the church. They went for a walk around the town park, the one adjacent to the church. They didn't talk very much; they just walked together.

Andy finally stopped crying, and they sat on a bench by one of the picnic tables.

"Feel better now?" Mr. Otis asked.

"Yes, thanks."

"Andy, I know Charlie liked you very much. It was just that he had a hard time showing it."

"He didn't used to."

"Well, I don't know. The two of you spent a lot of time together. Maybe he thought he shouldn't be hanging around a kid your age so much."

Andy didn't understand why anyone would think he shouldn't hang around Charlie, but he didn't pursue the matter and changed the subject.

"Now that Charlie's gone and Dad has sold our herd, I won't have a job for summer. Do you think I could drive your herd this summer?"

"I'd like that Andy, but you see I'm going to sell my herd too. I'm old, and it's getting pretty hard for me to keep up with the work. And," he said with a smile, "I'd like to take it easy for a while before it's my turn."

"Are you going to stay in town?"

"Well, I don't think so. Ruby wants to move to the city to be nearer her sister, and I wouldn't mind living there either," Mr. Otis replied. "Besides, there isn't much here for me anymore. All my friends have died. Charlie and me were the last."

When they parted, Mr. Otis shook Andy's hand and told him he was always welcome to come for a visit whenever he was in the city. Andy thanked him.

Dad couldn't find a farmer to buy the land so the same firm that bought the Otis farmland also bought the Parker's land. They said they intended to lease the land to farmers for a few years, but the town could look forward to a whole new shopping area that would rival the one in the city. There would be a new housing development that would nearly double the size of the town.

For the next few weeks Andy watched as the relatives he didn't know gradually hauled away the furniture and household items from Charlie's house. A "for sale" sign was attached to the fence by the front gate, and everything, including the lace curtains and green blinds in the living room, was stripped out of the house. A trailer was backed up to the front gate, and boxes and cans laden with things that no one wanted were hauled away.

By mid-May all the animals were sold, and a young couple from out of town with two young kids moved into the house. They painted it yellow.

XXI

On the Saturday before school let out for the summer, Andy and Ray were playing at the upper canal by the dump. They played all morning by the canal and, although it was still too cold to swim, they had fun making sailboats and planning again for a camping trip for the weekend following the 4th of July.

Tired of the boats, they crossed the fence and slid down the embankment to the old gravel pit that now served as the town garbage dump. Lots of good stuff was discarded during spring-cleaning time, and there were boxes of things that had been recently thrown out everywhere.

Andy was looking through a large cardboard box full of old magazines, and Ray searched in a box of old wrapping paper and ribbons when he discovered something wrapped in tissue paper.

"Andy, come and see what I found," Ray yelled over to him.

Andy threw down the magazine and climbed over some boxes to where Ray was unwrapping something. "What is it?" Andy asked.

"It looks like a horse somebody carved out of wood," Ray said, "but it's got a leg broken off."

Andy paused. Where had he seen that horse before? "Do you want it then?"

"Naw, you can have it if you'll give me that green bottle you found," Ray said.

"Okay," Andy said and they swapped items. "Is the broken off leg in that tissue paper?"

"I didn't see it."

Andy laid the horse on an upturned five-gallon can and rummaged through the box of wrapping paper. In the bottom of the box he found the piece of the hind leg. He fit it to the horse and it matched perfectly. He could repair the fracture and make the horse as good as new.

He left Ray at his front gate. Across the street Fred Olsen and a crew of workmen were tearing down the Lambert barn. Andy waved to them. He had heard someone from out of town bought the back half of the Lambert's yard, and since the Lambert's barn was no longer used, they planned to tear it down and build a house on the spot.

Andy went home with his treasure under his arm. He had wrapped the piece of the hind leg in tissue paper and tucked it safely in his back pocket.

He hadn't even gotten his skates out of the box in the basement this spring. He didn't feel like skating. Maybe he was getting too old for that kind of stuff.

Perspiration glistened on his forehead from the hot sun, and he squinted his eyes to reduce the glare from the sun on the sidewalk. Andy didn't remember it ever being so hot this early in the summer. The town was strangely quiet. There was no birdsong. There were lots of birds up by the canal where the willows grew, but there didn't seem to be many birds in town, not even in the orchards. The town sure looked different without the poplars, and it was hot.

It didn't take long for Andy to repair the horse's broken leg. He glued it in position and, after the glue dried, he sanded off the excess. When he had finished rubbing on the oil that Dad gave him, the horse looked as good as new.

Andy slouched in the porch swing. The evening shadows stretched full length from the red maples, but they couldn't compare to the deep and gigantic shadows the poplars cast. There sure wasn't much shade anymore. Without the trees and with so many barns being torn down, the town didn't look like it used to. The whole place was ugly and Andy didn't want to live here anymore.

He wiped his forehead and placed the repaired wooden horse on the porch floor in front of him. It was beautifully carved. What was it about that horse? And then he remembered. It looked like Ben's bronze horse, only this one was even better. It was a magnificent animal and well worth the scolding Mom gave him when he brought it home. Andy knew exactly where he would put it in his room. Maybe he could create something as wonderful some day.

THE END

Also available from PublishAmerica

A DEER IN WINTER
by Michelle Ordynans

A Deer in Winter is an inspiring story of survival. It's the semi-autobiographical tale of a young woman's odyssey as she escapes from an abusive home, endures homelessness in the cold of a New York winter, and survives sexual attacks and harassment. In the meantime, she continues her last term of high school while secretly homeless, in constant fear of being discovered and returned to her abusive household. Through it all, she sets her sights on meeting her ultimate goal—graduating high school and attending college in the fall so that she can eventually rise above her troubled background and build a better life for herself. All the rituals of daily life must be negotiated: how and where she sleeps each night, in the rain and snow; how she gets food; how she cleans herself and her clothes; and how she spends her evenings. Along the way she works, makes friends and boyfriends, and explores the fascinating sites of New York City.

Paperback, 206 pages
6" x 9"
ISBN 1-4241-6999-2

About the author:

Michelle Ordynans was born and has lived in New York most of her life, with her early childhood in Florida and a few years in Israel. She is married and has two grown children and several pets. She works with her husband and son as an insurance broker in New York City.

Available to all bookstores nationwide.
www.publishamerica.com

Also available from PublishAmerica

TUNNEL OF DARKNESS
by Rose Falcone De Angelo

Why are some people given the ability
to see into the future or communicate
with the dead? Is this a gift or a curse?
The visions come uninvited and change
an ordinary world into one of marvel,
turmoil and sometimes fear. This is the
story of Bernadette, whose psychic
powers begin at the age of ten and carry
her into the strangest places.

Paperback, 241 pages
6" x 9"
ISBN 1-60474-153-8

About the author:

Rose Falcone De Angelo was born in New York City's east side to
Italian immigrant parents. Rose moved to Florida in 1986. She is
the author of a book of poetry, *Reality and Imagination*. At ninety-
one, she is the oldest published poet in the state of Florida and has
intrigued all who have the privilege of knowing her. She is currently
working on her memoirs.

Available to all bookstores nationwide.
www.publishamerica.com